Black Rose

Grace Scott

I dedicate this book to my parents.

Book I: Jin's Requiem

Self-proclaimed Detective Jin Tohari

He was so close to catching her! Sixteen-year-old self-proclaimed detective, Jin Tohari groaned in frustration as he chased the black silhouette in front of him. That mysterious Black Rose drove him mad! Every time there was a crime, she was there beating the police to the scene and saving the day. Jin was amazed, not to mention a little suspicious, of the young crime fighter who always seemed to know where and when something was going to happen. She called herself Black Rose and did things no normal person could do. Of course, according to her everything she did was normal. *Jin* was the strange one for not being able to jump from buildings and disappear into thin air. And according to his sources (Jin being one of them) Black Rose had almost *magical* abilities. Utter nonsense to Jin, of course. Magic was fairytale, children's stories, nothing more and none of that sort of thing was real. The self-proclaimed detective did not believe in magic. Not at first, not before meeting Black Rose. But he started having second thoughts when it came to her.

Something flew past Jin's head, slicing his cheek so it bled. He stumbled to a stop and look behind him. A single black rose stuck in the pavement as if it were planted there all along. Jin was too deep into the chase to be surprised by this toy of hers. He whipped back around, glaring. Who could make attacking flowers out of thin air and honestly call themselves normal?

Jin ran forward; ready to get some answers out of the mysterious girl.

He watched Black Rose sprint forward and leap onto the roof of a neighboring building. The tail of her black coat flapped in the air and her boots made a clicking noise as she landed gracefully. Jin grunted and quickly followed after her. He had to find out who she was!

Jin made a running start and jumped over the space between buildings. He landed on the roof and rolled to cushion his fall. Jin recovered quickly and his eyes began searching for Black Rose. As soon as he saw her, a tornado of midnight rose petals attacked him. He made a shield with his arms to cover his face and winced when one of the petals cut his skin. Within seconds, the force of the petals knocked Jin off his feet and he landed on his back. His eyes widened when he heard a giggle. Jin shot up and looked around wildly for the figure.

"What was that for?" Jin cried when he spotted Black Rose. The self-proclaimed detective stumbled onto his feet. Black Rose smiled.

"You won't give up, will you?"

"Why would I?" Jin questioned. "I saw you running away from the bank robbery two days ago! Do you have something to hide?"

If Jin noticed correctly, Black Rose's composure changed a little.

"What about it?" she asked. "You *cannot* blame me for that!"

"The cops don't know where the money is and *I* saw you! Where's the money?"
Black Rose scowled.

"Your eyes mean nothing at all to them," she said. "So why are you bothering?"
Jin folded his arms over his chest and huffed.

"My eyes are helping them," he snapped, but a smirk slowly spread across his lips. His feet kept moving, inching closer to Black Rose. She was *letting* him get close.

"...But then again, you seem to have many eyes all over the city," he said. "I wonder, are they all that pretty shade of brown?"

"Flattery isn't working," Black Rose replied just as quickly.

This was getting him nowhere and it became annoying after weeks of the same thing.

"Let's cut the crap, tell me who you are! And who took the money!" Jin shouted.

Black Rose let out a short laugh and wagged a finger at Jin.

"Why don't you have your *uncle* look for it in the old hideout? I am sure *they* left it there."

Jin took his last step forward so that he was a few feet away from Black Rose, but then the blizzard or petals started barreling into him once more. The razor sharp petals cut his skin once more and Jin winced on pain. This was getting out of hand! Jin rolled out of the way and charged forward, watching as Black Rose jumped to the edge of the roof. Her back was to the horizon, setting her black clad figure aglow with golden-orange sunlight. Jin bit back the urge to remain breathless. A stray petal cut the skin between his middle and pointer finger, bringing him back to reality. Jin shuddered.

"Why should I believe you?" Jin shouted, cradling his bleeding hand. "I know you are the thief!"

"Then I must admit, you do not know much," Black Rose said before sighing in a disappointed sort of way. "Do me a favor and stop following me around. Stupid people like you are hardly any fun."

"When I unmask you, then we'll see who will have all the fun," Jin growled, furious at all the insults.

Black Rose laughed again and rose petals started again. Jin was starting to hate thin air. If the air was thick would she still be able to create monster petals from it? Jin pushed forward, ignoring the pain, until he was right in front of her. Jin lifted on of his wounded hands and held her cheek in his palm. His heart was pounding in wild exhilaration and excitement. Black Rose was in his grasp! Something inside of Jin quivered at the smoothness and warmth of Black Rose's skin.

"Stay a while," Jin said inching closer. "Unless you have something to hide?"

"So sorry, but I have... other engagements," Black Rose said with a smirk on her face. Without warning, she closed her eyes and fell over the edge of the roof. Jin's eyes widened as he fell with her. Exhilaration gone, fear started to slam into his body as cold air whipped his face. Black Rose laughed and Jin saw her disappear into the darkness. Jin screamed, fear now overriding his system as the pavement neared his head.

He was going to die!

A gust of air shot Jin back up, suddenly causing his eyes to tear. His body shot up over the edge of the building and landed roughly back down. His body was trembling and his breath came out in loud pants. Jin could not move because he still felt as if he were flying through the air.

"Leave me alone," Black Rose's voice echoed though the night. "You should be smart enough to understand that."

"Black Rose!" he shouted into the air. Nothing replied back. Jin yelled in frustration before he pounded his fist against the roof. She was just playing with him! Jin continued to slam his fist against the roof until his hand became sore. She was playing him like some sort of game! He could not belive it. After weeks of chasing her, she finally showed her ture colors. Jin wanted to curse this new turn of events when a voice in the back of his head told him to get his anger under control. Jin steadied his breathing and calmed his racing heart. He rolled onto his back and stood up.

"She's insane..." he muttered. He was surprised his heart did not give out because of sheer fright this evening. But something about the sensations she gave him caused him to want more. It was like the excitement from it all begged his mind and body for more. After the fright left the desire to finally catch her, the rip the mast off her. It was if she opened up a new Jin- a Jin he was sure he knew nothing about. But this excited him even more. Jin wondered if he caused the same thing inside of Black Rose.

"One day," Jin vowed, "one day Black Rose I'll find out who you are and you'll tell me everything."

Jin scanned the darkening skyline for a few more seconds before turning around. A tall wall surrounded all of Hainai District. It stretched and passed out of Jin's sight. The wall was a constant reminder that there were things outside of Hainai District that the people wanted to keep a secret. Beyond the wall, it was barren and nothing good came out of going out of Hainai. Jin was told never to go out of the city. But unlike everyone else in Hainai District, Jin wanted to know what was out there. He wanted to know everything his parents did about the outside world. Why did everyone in Hainai think that the outside world was a dangerous place? Could it be worse than the vilest places in Hainai? Jin stared at the wall for a few more seconds, deep in thought.

Jin looked towards the doorway to the stairs, when he heard a banging noise from within. The door slammed open and four people came running out with guns raised. When they noticed no one was on the roof except Jin, they lowered their weapons and let someone through.

Oh no. Jin thought.

Tekeda Tohari was a man of average height and weight and was middle aged. He had brown eyes and black hair that he slicked back. His beard was neatly trimmed and that added to his 'second look' handsomeness. He wore a tan trench coat and a blue scarf, but his customary tan hat was not placed on his head. The commissioner had a stern look upon his face as he noticed Jin.

"Where'd she go?" Tekeda asked. "Did that girl escape again?"

Jin nodded, looking in the direction where Black Rose jumped from the roof. A couple of men walked over to where Jin pointed.

"Yeah," he muttered.

"Darn it! How in the world does she manage to get to things we don't?" Tekeda questioned angrily. "Did she say anything to you? What about the stolen money? Did she have it?"

Jin looked back at his uncle nodding.

"She said that the money was in the old hideout the thieves used... that was it," he replied.

"We checked that place already," Tekeda muttered. He raised his hand to his hair and ruffled it slightly. Jin looked at his uncle while he thought. His uncle was the top of the police force in Hainai District. Yet recently, Tekeda was distressed because of Jin and his need to find out exactly who the mysterious Black Rose girl was.

Black Rose was different from the normal criminals of Hainai District and Tekeda had a feeling she was not from Hainai at all. If that were true, that would mean she was potentially dangerous. All outer worlders were dangerous. Tekeda Tohari turned to his men.

"Go search the Luxefore lot! Don't leave a thing unturned!" he barked. The Hainai District Police turned heel and ran back down the stairs. Tekeda looked behind his shoulder at his nephew.

"Go straight home Jin and clean yourself up. You look a mess," he said gruffly, eyeing his nephew up and down. "And be careful."

Jin nodded, not in the mood to dispute. He lost Black Rose again and she was even within arms length this time! Jin fumed as he walked down the staircase of the building and on to the streets of Hainai District's Hainai City. It was the largest place in Hainai that was populated. The city had tall buildings blocking the sky with nightlights flashing, stores in stores on stores- everything the people loved. Jin thought he was supposed to be in the middle of it all, but every time he took it into consideration he found that he liked open spaces more. He loved chasing Black Rose over the tall buildings because the rooftops opened up to the night sky. Jin was allowed to be exhilarated and free on the rooftops but as soon as he was brought back by reality, he found himself on the streets of Hainai, closed in and isolated.

Not many people were out on the street this evening. A cautious hush whispered around the streets now. *Probably because of the raid*, Jin thought as he made his way to the train station. Here he was, a sixteen-year-old boy walking down the streets alone. Of course because of the raid, he was never *really* alone. Police lined every street from Main to the White Cloud Square. And being the police commissioner's nephew helped.

Hainai was strange. It was safe, but unsafe at the same time. Jin knew the streets not to go on, knew what time he was the safest in the city, and when the high ciminal activity was. Even so, he was grateful for the people who were robbed, kidnapped and even those who occasionally impersonated outer worlders. It gave him something to do. It gave him a reason to chase Black Rose.

*   *   *

"How many times have I asked you *not* to go looking after Black Rose?" Tekeda asked fuming. His nephew ignored him, while he looked at old paper clippings and black and white photos.

"Are you listening to me?" Tekeda asked.

Jin flipped a photograph over and scribbled something on the back of it.

"*You're* the one who told me not to give up the chase," Jin countered.

Tekeda made a move to push all the papers off his nephew's bed, but Jin slapped his hand on his belongings and glared at his uncle.

"I'm not giving this up!"
Tekeda sighed.

"This is just some silly game right now Jin," he said. "You'll forget about it once you stop."
Jin's face did not change and neither did his resolve.

"You don't understand and I don't expect you to! She saved *Aya*! But there is so much more to her than that! I *need* to know why she does what she does!" Jin cried angrily. "You do what you need to do and I'll do what I need to!"

"I don't want you getting hurt! How am I supposed to concentrate on my duties, if I'm worried about your welfare?" Tekeda cried angrily. "What will I say to your parents then?"

Jin let out a frustrated groan and turned his head to the side. He ran his fingers through his mess of spiky raven hair letting the disappointment of the night's chase free. He looked at his uncle again with a calmer expression and nodded.

"If I get hurt, it will be my fault," Jin said. "Let me be the one to deal with the consequences."

There was a tense minute of silence and Jin thought that his uncle was going to argue with him again, but Tekeda just made a gruff noise and turned around.

"I'll continue this in the morning," he said before walking through the door. Jin nodded and continued his work. He knew his uncle would not continue the conversation until another time... morning not being one of them.

Jin scrutinized the belongings on his bed. The notebook at his side was filled with notes about Black Rose and all the things she did and could possibly do. The images on his bed were a mixture of quick shots of Black Rose in action (none of them were clear), and drawings of Black Rose made by one of Jin's friends. The paper clippings were from the newspaper with articles about Black Rose.
Jin flipped some articles sighing angrily.

"How am I supposed to find you if you keep-"

Jin's thigh vibrated and he jumped slightly. He dug into his pocket and pulled out a small box. Jin opened the small box lid and a little glowing globe popped up.

"It's Jin," Jin answered. "Erick! What's up?"
Jin listened to his friend's voice for a moment.

"Another one?" Jin asked. "You need to make another sketch? What'd she look like? Hm..."

Jin thought for a moment.

"She had high boots on today, and this black coat, yeah, like a trench, yeah, with a tail. No, it was black on the inside too. No, today her hair was black and long- wavy too. Uh-huh. Her eyes were- yeah! How'd you know? She always wears that black mask... Did you find something out?"
Jin listened in silence for a few more seconds.

"Whaddya mean, you'll tell me tomorrow?" he cried. "What good are you, man? Geez."
Jin was silent for a few more seconds.

"Of course, I still think she's the Chang girl!"
Jin was silent.

"Why wouldn't I believe you? Of *course* you're right about the similarities! She hides a lot too and every time I mention Black Rose around her, she—I know! She clams right up! She's making me pry! What did you say you...! I am *not* obsessed!"
Jin had a frown on his face.

"I've told you before I don't really *know* why I... I just do! I have a feeling that's all..." Jin listened for a little while. "You laugh, that's why I don't explain it to you, stupid... It's called a *feeling*."

Jin made a very unpleasant face and listened to his friend's voice.

"Yeah, I'll see you tomorrow," he finally said. "Bye."

Jin closed the box lid and the glowing sphere disappeared. He flopped onto his bed exhausted. Erick Bastion was his best friend who was interested in trying to find out who Black Rose really was. He was the artist that did all the drawings of Black Rose. He helped paint a picture of Black Rose's secret identity. Even though they were friends, Erick had a way of making Jin embarrassed in a way no one else could. He also found a way to make Jin realize how much work he needed to get finished.

"Jin Tohari, it looks like you have a long way to go," Jin sighed. He packed all his work up and readied himself for bed. He would challenge Chang the next day and see if she would give in. Jin turned off his light and made himself comfortable.

I am not obsessed… He thought in a slightly bitter tone as he drifted off to sleep. For weeks, the desire to catch her lingered in his body. It flowed to his fingertips every night she appeared. And tonight, he hand the pleasure of touching her after so long. Jin sighed.

He was not obsessed. It was so much more than than that… whatever *that* was.

Xia

Xia Chang walked to school with the customary 'don't-talk-to-me' look planted firmly on her pretty face. A few schoolmates, with large duffle bags on their shoulders, passed without even the slightest hello. Xia did not care. It was better if they did not know her. That way, she would not have to worry about them getting in her way. With her occupation, she had no time or room for mistakes. Xia walked past a shop and glanced at herself in the large window. Average height, pale skin, dark brown eyes, light brown hair. Almost everything about her was different. Xia looked at the other students walking ahead of her. They were different from her- rather she was different from them. They smiled and laughed and cried. They had so many faces. Xia slowly continued walking in the direction of her school. She began to wonder how people could manage all the faces they put on.

The mountainous Meadow Street meant instant exhaustion to all South Hainai District High School students. It was one of the longest slopes in Hainai District and ended right into the school's courtyard. Xia stopped walking once she reached the top of the street. She turned around and gazed over the wall surrounding the whole town. She was different because she was from out there. Outside the wall was a world completely different from Hainai District. The people here had no idea what was out there and they had no desire to. Hainai District was its own little world- its own little bubble of humanity on something much greater.

A small ringer and vibration made Xia dig into her plaid skirt uniform's pocket. She pulled out a black and white patterned box and opened the cover. A sphere popped up. She was sent a message from her mother. After reading it, she closed the box lid and continued her walk to school. She had a meeting with the Organization today. It was not something she was looking forward to. They always made her want to quit. Xia knew very well that she could not quit the Organization. It was not her choice to be part of the Organization, she was born into it. The least she could do was make sure her weight was accounted for, no matter how much she did not want to at times.

"How much longer will it take for me to complete my training?" Xia asked herself as she walked down the sloping street to school.

Xia arrived at South Hainai District High and avoided the few students that were already there by heading straight for the gymnasium. She placed her duffle bag down on the bench in the locker room and changed into her practice leotard and shorts. She locked her things in her locker and entered the gym. She sat on a mat and started to stretch her limbs, releasing the tension that had built in place there. After continuing for fifteen minutes, Xia stood up and walked to the pull up bars and started with fifteen chin-ups. She had to focus on her day. She could not afford distractions.

"Class, put your books away. We need to vote for the school trip!"

Class 1-A cheered. The school trip was the highlight of the year and choosing it was the best part. Xia looked at the class with detached interest. She would have preferred to stay in school rather than go on the trip. How was she supposed to do her job if she was away? Mr. A took out a stack of sheets and handed them to Xia.

"Would you mind passing these out, Miss Chang?" he asked.

Xia looked up from her thoughts, and nodded. She stood up and started passing out the lists of places to choose from. There was an excited murmur around the room as the class began to decide where they wanted to go. Everything was going by smoothly until Xia passed the desk of a boy in her class. Xia could not be less excited to walk by his desk and give him a trip sheet. She did her best to keep her straight face up when handing the offending person the paper, but in reality she wanted to give him a nice paper cut across his extended hand.

Jin Tohari looked up at Xia, grinning. Xia's eye twitched in annoyance. How she hated the boy sitting oh-so-smugly in front of her.

"Did you know that a *black rose* symbolizes rebirth in death?" Jin said grinning and taking the paper. "I think it's really a beautiful flower."

Xia stared at Jin for a moment, before turning away. She did not need to hear the rest of what he was saying to understand what he was implying. Xia handed out the rest of the forms and sat down to complete her own. Without looking at it much Xia picked the first option. Her jaw was tight and she had to force herself to relax. Every time the Tohari boy opened his mouth, she would get upset. She would lose her cool. Xia hated losing her cool, calm and collected composure. It was the one thing she could rely on in her world.

"Has everyone finished?" Mr. A asked.

The class chanted a 'yes'. Xia walked around and picked up the trips sheets. The class started to talk once more about the trip and what they chose. Xia reached Jin Tohari's desk and he handed her the sheet without saying anything this time around. He still had that grin on his face that made Xia think about wiping off. It seemed taunting and secretive-made just for her. Every time she looked at him she got annoyed. And for her, that was unacceptable.

After giving the papers to Mr. A, Xia sat back down in her seat. She looked out the window while Mr. A started tallying the requests. The cheers and moans from the class all became background noise to Xia, as she looked past the school grounds and to the gate to the outside world. It looked barren, like a desert but she knew that was a trick. Hainai District was like a little bubble and all the people who lived here were ignorant to the bigger things controlling their lives.

"We have a winner!" Mr. A announced and the class stopped talking and looked at the board. Xia stopped looking out the window and looked at the front too. She wanted to know where she was going to be tortured for an entire weekend.

"The Winterwonderland seems to be the place that everyone wants to go to," Mr. A said. Xia blanched. Of all the places to be picked, the class had to pick that one. It was going to be cold and everyone was going to be out together sipping hot chocolates and hogging the hot springs. The class cheered loudly. Mr. A smiled and told the class that he was going to the main office to deliver the papers. The class was almost over anyway, and the students in 1-A were taught everything they were going to learn for that period. Because of that, the rest of the period was going to be free. Some students started to walk around the room and talk to one another.

Xia turned her head to look out the window and was face to face with someone's midsection. Jerking her head back Xia looked up at the person responsible for blocking her window space.

"Tohari," she said in a calm but firm voice, "can I help you with something?"

"No, not really," Jin said sitting on Xia's desk. "I just wanted to ask you where you chose to go."
Xia glared at Jin hoping it would make him disappear.

"It doesn't matter," Xia said shortly.

Xia turned her head to look at the door since Jin's backside was in her way.

"That's rude Xia! We're *talking*!"
Xia scowled.

"We would not be if you just shut your mouth," she muttered. "Can you leave me alone? *Now* preferably?"

Jin laughed and scooted closer to Xia and she abruptly stood up. The bell rang and it was time for the next class. Xia moved from her desk as fast as she could, doing her best not to be the last one in the room.

Her eyes widened slightly. The last person just left the room. They cleared out faster than Xia had hoped.

"My, isn't this cozy?" Jin said. Xia wanted to kill someone because they left her in the same room as Jin Tohari.

"No," Xia muttered angrily. She willed her feet to move quickly towards the door. Jin grabbed her hand.

"Where are you going?" he asked. "We haven't finished our conversation."

Xia wrenched her hand out of Jin's, disliking the contact to the point of revulsion.

"What makes you think you can touch me like that?" Xia glared menacingly at Jin. He just held his cocky grin in place.

"I'll see you in gym," he said waving, as Xia stormed out of the classroom.

No good, spiky haired idiot! Xia thought furiously as she walked to her class. On the outside she seemed cool, but inside she was raging.

Why won't he just leave me out of his stupid schemes! Okay relax, relax Xia. That Tohari boy cannot get the better of you! Breathe Xia, breathe. Xia thought and started to control her breathing. As she walked into her next class, she was the refined cool Xia she had always been and always wanted to be.

"Oh my goodness! Look!" An excited cry came from classroom 1-C. The class crowded close to the window looking down at the basketball courts. Yells came from the hallway and down from the court.

"Tohari and Chang are at it again!"

Xia hated him more than ever during gym class. It was a simple game of dodge ball. No one was going to get injured, as long as they were not Tohari. Xia gripped her ball tighter. He touched her! *What gave him the right?* Xia felt her anger grow. She had to remain calm and focus on the game, focus on getting Tohari back for his comments.

"Okay, Tohari, Chang this is to be a *fair game*. Do your best not to kill one another, please?" Joe Kane, physical education teacher at South Hainai High School, pleaded.

"Let's go, Kane!" Jin said. "I want to beat Chang to the ground."

"Do not flatter yourself," Xia muttered.

Joe pleaded some more but his words were unheard by the students. Xia concentrated on Jin, ready to pound him with the ball. Her frustration would be let out in a productive way and Jin would spend the rest of the afternoon in the infirmary. It would be very productive indeed.

The whistle blew and the gym class began. Within a few minutes, most of the students were contented to get out and watch to avoid injury.

Xia jumped back from getting hit and blocked a ball with the one she was holding. She saw Tohari running for a ball and threw her ball at the one on the ground. It popped from Tohari's grasp and just in time he jerked back from one aimed at his feet. Xia picked up another ball and was ready to throw it, but she noticed two balls flying at her and dived to avoid them. She threw the ball into the air to deflect another ball aimed at her. Her fingers just managed not to get jammed in the way of a falling ball and she caught it as it bounced up and threw it hard. Tohari's face was in shock as the ball whizzed past his head.

"*Fair play!*" Joe yelled, but winced when a ball flew past Xia's head.

Xia turned angry eyes toward Jin. The game was never going to stop. Not until Tohari and his pretty little face were pummeled. The students around the battlefield were cheering loudly. They made Xia's resolve stronger. She picked up a ball and threw it, dodged one, threw one, blocked one, threw one, dived for cover. No one made her this competitive and she did not like it. She did not like it when she lost her cool. Suddenly, a ball flew into her stomach and Xia doubled over in pain.

No! How could this have happened? She thought as she clutched her stomach. Xia looked up to see Tohari in the same position she was, looking equally horrified.

When did I get hit? When did I hit him? Xia thought, slowly getting up.

Joe ran to the court to see if either of his students was injured. Neither of them were hurt much, physically at least. Their egos however…

"Because you were both hit at the exact same time, you both are out in a tie!" Joe said smiling. *"Thank goodness!"*

Xia glared at Tohari and he glared back. They would settle this oneday. The class was in awe and cheered loudly. Chatter broke out loudly about battle between Xia and Jin. Xia sat out and tried to watch everything but her gym class, for the remainder of the period.

It was a little chilly out but the cool breeze felt nice against her hot skin. A gust of wind blew her long ponytail of light brown hair against her face and she moved to get it out of her eyes. She turned against the wind.

Her dark brown eyes locked with honey colored ones.

Why was Jin Tohari looking at her like that?

*   *   *

Xia walked home after gymnastics club. Her practise routine had to be perfect. She had to do her best and her best had to be perfect. Xia closed her eyes and let the wind blow past her as she stood still. Where did the wind touch when it passed Hainai's walls? Xia opened her eyes and imagined herself away from Hainai and in the outer world.

A strong gust of wind shoved Xia forward into something sturdy with a mass of spiky black hair.

"I am sorry the wind-" Xia started but stopped short when she looked up. Jin Tohari was looking down at Xia with

17

a surprised expression on his face. His strong hands were on her forearms keeping her upright. Another gust blew, before Xia could say anything and pushed her closer to Jin. Everything was against her! She was too upset and embarrassed to even say anything to the annoying boy! She was in enemy hands! Her nice walk home was not supposed to go on like this!

The wind finally stopped and Xia quickly removed herself from Jin's grasp. She stumbled away from Jin and began walking home again. She could not bring herself to even look at him.

"What, no thanks?"

Xia walked as quickly as she could towards her home.

"I'll remember this, Chang!" Jin called.

Xia wanted to forget the moment ever happened.

Warmth

Xia carried her school bag in her hand and her gymnastics duffle on her shoulder. A group of police hovercrafts were parked, sloppily, in an apartment complex in downtown Hainai City known as Luxefore Lot. Xia noticed three officers fully armed, escorting one of the main gang leaders out of the complex. She felt the edges of her mouth turn upward in as much of a grin as she would dare manage on a normal basis. If she did any more of the work, the Hainai Police would be bored and she did not want that. They already would not leave her alone. Especially Jin Tohari. That boy was far keener than his uncle and no matter how careful she was, he would always be on her heels, confronting her about things she did not do. Xia sighed, not wanting to think about Jin, and walked across the street to two idle police officers.

"Excuse me officers, could you tell me what happened?" Xia asked politely.

"Confidential information Miss," one of the officers replied curtly.

Xia frowned.

"But it is for the journalism club in my school. Could you at least give me the kiddy version?" she questioned testing out her pleading look. She never used it before but it seemed to work.

"Alright, but no names," the other officer said.

"That doesn't make for a very good paper..." Xia muttered trying to look disappointed.

"No names," the second officer said firmly. "You're a writer, be creative."

Xia sighed.

"Fine," she said.

The officers smiled.

19

"A group of thugs just got caught with a lot of stolen money," the first officer explained.

"Right, the "Andez" right?" Xia questioned. When the officers gave her looks she quickly smiled. "I watch a lot of news," she amended.

"Right," the first officer said with questioning in his tone of voice. "Well one Andez member escaped but don't worry the police are handling it very well."

"I see," Xia said. "Did anything happen with that one who escaped?"

"Why do you say that?" the second officer questioned, obviously suspicious.
Xia shrugged.

"Well just with their pattern crime," she replied. "I would think they would leave something to taunt the police like usual."
The first officer bristled.

"I can assure you the police will have the last laugh," he said angrily. Xia smiled apologetically.

"Of course they will!" Xia said, trying to sound excited. "Commissioner Tohari always gets things done! I remember when-"

"Right well, the one who escaped left a note for Black Rose," the second officer said. Xia's eyes narrowed slightly. They left a note for Black Rose? This was interesting and Xia was going to demand more information.

"Black Rose? Isn't she that new teen heroine? She's so cool!" Xia said imitating a normal, excited teenage girl. Her jaw was hurting from smiling so much.

"Black Rose is a menace! If she is on our side than she should either reveal herself of turn herself in!" the second officer said.

"But she's only helped you guys," Xia muttered sounding like an annoyed fan of Black Rose. There were so many of them in South Hainai that Xia knew how to look and sound like them.

"She's from the outer world and all outer worlders are dangerous!" the second police officer snapped. Xia frowned and steadied her racing heart. She needed to compose herself. No need to cause suspicion.

"Right, so what did the note say?" Xia asked returning to the topic of the note left for Black Rose.

"You're awfully interested in this Miss..." the first officer trailed at her name.

"Jae," Xia snapped annoyed. "Now what did the note say?"

The first officer smirked.

"Jae was it?" the first officer shared a look with the second. The second officer excused herself and walked in the direction of the other policemen.

"So what school do you go to?" the first officer asked.

"South Hainai," Xia muttered. She knew the other officer was going to see if her name was real and the one in front of her was stalling to waste time. The whole business annoyed her.

"Look, if you don't tell me, I'll go to Jin," Xia said smoothly. Her balled into a fist when his name left her lips. The thought of saying it repulsed her and after having said if so familiarly, Xia was certain she would die on the spot. The mere implication that she was that acquainted with Jin Tohari made her sick to her stomach.

"You know Jin Tohari?" the officer questioned cautiously.

Xia smiled, feeling the words in her throat burn it.

"Yeah, we're the best of friends!"

The officer looked skeptical, at best. Xia milked the lie for all it was worth, before she had to flee because of her sickness.

"I know all about his detective adventures. He tells me everything about them," she said. "So I know he'll find out what is on that note and I'll just ask him then."

"Ask me what, Eunmi Jae?"

21

Xia felt a hand on her body and her whole body froze. Less than a second later Jin Tohari was standing by her side with a smirk on his lips and his hand resting on her waist. Xia wondered just how long he had been listening and where he was listening from.

"If you could possibly remove your hand from my waist," Xia muttered through gritted teeth. "I said we were the best of friends not best of friends with benefits."

Jin laughed and slowly removed his hand from Xia's waist. His fingers slid across the small of her back and a tremble ran through Xia. She glared at the spiky-haired boy, who looked as if he did nothing wrong. Xia fought almost everything she had to smack Jin across his cheek. The other part of her knew that the police officer was looking at her carefully, making sure she was who she claimed to be.

"So what were you saying about Black Rose?" Jin asked the police officer.

"The note that was left for her," the officer replied. "Miss Jae wanted to know of its contents."

"Lucky you! I've already found what the note said," Jin smiled at Xia who smiled back. She could not believe that she was receiving aid from Jin, let alone smile at him. She never smiled and yet in one day it seemed she was forced to.

"Lucky me!" Xia said forcing herself to laugh. Out of the corner of her eye she saw the other police pointing in her direction. She had to move on quickly. She grabbed Jin's hand and proceeded to walk away with him.

"Tell me all about it!" she said excitedly. "Thanks for your time officer!"

Jin laughed and let Xia drag him down the hill. As soon as they were out of sight Xia released Jin's hand as if it were on fire, and rubbed her sore cheeks. She wanted to scream, or punch a wall, something to release the pent up frustration. She smiled at Jin, held his hand, said she was his friend and did not slap him for touching her so familiarly! Xia balled her hand into a fist to keep herself in check.

"You're a good actress," Jin's voice came to her ears. "And you have such a pretty smile. Who knew?"

Xia turned around to face Jin, her expressionless mask back in place.

"What did the note say?" Xia asked ignoring Jin's compliments.

Jin sighed.

"Must you rush things?" he replied with another dramatic sigh.

Xia could not take anymore. She grabbed Jin by his uniform's tie and slammed him against the wall. The boy did not wince but kept Xia's gaze just as fiercely. The smirk on his lips annoyed Xia even more.

"I've been far too nice to you," she growled. "Tell me what the note said or I will hurt you."

Jin's grin widened.

"Whether I tell you or not, you'll find out won't you?" he asked. "But I'm honored you want me to tell you."

Xia glared murderously at him and shoved him against the wall again before walking away from him. Her body was tense with anger and she hated having to do everything the hard way when the easy was being difficult. She heard Jin laugh before she felt his hand slip into hers.

"Black Rose is to meet the Andez is the third space tonight," Jin said, holding Xia still with his free hand, "and she is to come at midnight."

Xia's heart jumped out of her chest. But the third space was the Luxefore lot! What were these people playing at? There was no way the place was going to be devoid of police activity by midnight. Xia's mind whirled but not enough to keep herself from noticing how close she was to Jin. His hand was in hers and the other was placed on her back once more. Somehow she managed be have her back against the wall she threw Jin against with Jin closer than she ever wanted him to be.

"Get away from me," Xia could not raise her voice because of the shock of being so close to him. "Get away from me, get away from me!"

"Relax," Jin said smoothly. "I won't bite...much."

"Jin!" Commissioner Tohari's voice made Xia jump slightly. Jin smirked and pulled away from Xia, but did not let her go.

"Uncle," Jin said smirking.
Tekeda sighed.

"Is that you're girlfriend?" he questioned. Xia felt a pang of furiousness enter her. She certainly was not Jin's girlfriend nor would she ever be!
Jin smiled.

"Of course," he said. Xia's eye twitched. She squeezed Jin's hand as hard as she could in anger.

"She said her surname was Jae," one of the officers from before said frowning.

"I lied," Xia said cutting off the officer before he could continue. "My name is Xia Chang."

"Ah, I thought so," Tekeda said. "You look just like your mother."
Xia did not say anything.

"What did you need?" Jin asked his uncle.

"Wanted to see who your girlfriend was," Tekeda replied. "Tell your father and mother yet?"
Jin shook his head.

"No, it happened while they were on excavation," Jin replied smoothly. "But I'll make sure they know."
Tekeda nodded and chuckled. He turned around and the other officer quickly followed him.

"They grow up so fast don't they?" he muttered to the other officer as they walked off. Jin chuckled and Xia quickly shrugged out of his grasp. She did not even want to think about how many times he touched her today!

"Your girlfriend?!" Xia cried, unable to keep her anger in check. "Who do you think you are? We have no such connection- nor will we ever!"

"How can you say that we'll *never* have that sort of relationship? I don't hate you at all and I'm sorry if I came off that way to you," Jin said, taking a step closer to Xia.

"*I* hate *you*!" Xia seethed. "The sooner you get that the better it will be for the both of us!"

Jin frowned.

"How can I possibly get myself to hate you, Black Rose?" Jin asked, his voice becoming softer. "And I know you don't hate me. You can't hate anyone."

Who did Jin think he was? Xia fist shook. She had never felt this angry in her entire life. She may not have really known what hate was, but Jin was sure to bring her to the right conclusion of it.

"I will assure you that I have no fond feelings for you," Xia spat. "Now leave me alone."

"No," Jin said. "I will not leave you. Not until you admit to being her."

Xia reeled her anger back in and her fist stop shaking.

"I am not Black Rose, Tohari," Xia said calmly. "Nor am I your girlfriend or friend for that matter."

Jin shook his head.

"Your denial only makes me think that you are," Jin said. He lifted his hand and it rested on Xia's cheek. Her eyes widened in anger and she slapped his hand away. She wanted to break all the fingers in that hand.

"How many times do I have to tell you not to touch me? Are you an idiot?" Xia snapped furiously.

"I *am* idiot, and you're very warm," Jin replied smiling, "much like Black Rose is."

Xia did not have the patience to take it. She turned around and quickly made her way to the train station. She was happy Jin did not follow her because she would have surely punched him in his face.

* * *

Xia paced in her room. She almost lost her composure completely. She nearly punched Jin in the face, and as satisfying as that would have been, he would have had the satisfaction of knowing that he could drive her over the edge. Xia could not have that, not when her training was at stake. Her pacing stopped.

"My training," she said in a soft voice.

Her training was more important than anything. If she allowed it to be hindered by some boy then she was not ready to fully join the Organization. No, she needed to find a way to outsmart him not only while she was Black Rose, but while she was Xia Chang as well. She needed to make sure Jin understood that she was not here for his entertainment. No at the most she was here to protect him… even if the prospect of a kidnapper kidnapping him and not rescuing him did sound appealing.

Xia looked up at her clock and noticed that it was ten minutes to midnight. How in the world would she manage to get inside of the Luxefore Lot without being noticed? Not to mention Jin would be there snooping around, waiting for her to come out so that he could chase her. Xia looked outside her window in thought. If there were some sort of door she could get into without being noticed this would be easier. But the Luxefore Lot cellar had long since been filled in and the rooftops were more likely to be locked and Xia was certain her transportation would not work because she had only been inside one room in the lot.

"Wait, that one room could give me access into the Lot," Xia said. "I just need to remember the details of it."

Xia frowned trying to remember what the room looked like exactly. She remembered a bed, and a chair by the window. Clothes were all over the ground and it smelled like dirt and money.

Xia grinned, feeling the pull of transportation hitting her. She subdued it and focused her magics on changing her appearance. Her jeans turned into a black skirt and shiny black boots. Her shirt was replaced with a long coat with red lining that fell to her knees. Xia opened her eyes and her mask was floating in front of her. She picked it up and put it on, transforming her hair midnight colored and wavy. She closed her eyes again and thought of the Luxefore Lot before her whole body disappeared from the room.

Black Rose's body appeared in the room she thought of and she was looking around before her feet hit the ground. No one was here and the Lot was eerily silent. Black Rose knew she had to make it to the inner courtyard in less than three minutes. She smirked. That was not going to be a problem considering this building was basically built the same way as all the other apartment complexes. Find the staircase and it leads to the basement and the basement led to the inner courtyard.

Black Rose made her way out of the room and found the door to the staircase. She looked down the space between railings and grinned. She was certain she could fit through there. Black Rose took a deep breath and hopped over the railing to the space in between them. Her body flew down toward the ground and she grinned. A foot above the floor below her, her body slowed down as her magics allowed her to float to the ground. As soon as her shoes clicked against tiled floor, Black Rose ran to the only open door in the basement that led to the inner courtyard: the back door.

Black Rose heard the sound of a chime in the distance signaling that it was midnight. Black Rose opened the back room and ran forward. She spilled onto a stone floor, and looked around. There was a tree in the center of the grassy yard with a glowing rope around it.

"Isn't it a little late for a midnight rendezvous?" she asked smoothly to a man waiting in the center by the tree.

"Is this not romantic? With a hostage and everything," the man said with a smile on his lips. Black Rose took a step forward and the man walked toward her. They met, with five feet between them.

"Let's get down to the point, Miss Rose," the man said. Black Rose raised an eyebrow. That was a new name to her. She did not like it.

"Let's," Black Rose said. "Let the hostage go, and I'll go easy on you."
The Andez member laughed.

"I want you dead," he said. "You completely destroyed my gang and I need revenge."

"I did not destroy your gang, the police did that," Black Rose said. "Now, untie the hostage or I'll do it after I finish you off."
The Andez pulled out a gun from his pocket and pointed it at Black Rose's head.

"We're so close I doubt I'll miss," the Andez member said grinning. Black Rose sighed and shook her head.

"Will you people never learn?" she asked. The Andez member shot a bullet and quicker than anything he had ever seen, Black Rose dodged it. She charged at him, kicking the weapon out of his hand. The looks of shock on their faces never got old to her. Black Rose's foot connected with the man's head and knocked him unconscious. Black Rose shook her head and ran to untie the hostage. To her utmost surprise there was no hostage waiting for her, but a bomb, ticking to go off in less than ten seconds.

"Curse you!" she cried as she ran back to the man and grabbed him just as the bomb exploded. Black Rose transported to outside of the building just as the flames licked her back.

Black Rose saw the looks of shock on the police force's faces when she landed in front of them with her clothes singed and an unconscious man in her arms. Her feet hit floor and Black Rose roughly tossed the Andez member down in front of the force.

"Take this idiot," she spat furiously. "I can't believe I fell for his trap!"

Black Rose was furious at herself. And a bomb, a bomb nearly killed her. How stupid was she to fall for that? There were no cries for help, no threats to kill the hostage, nothing like that. Black Rose's fist shook and she took off down the street before anyone could question her.

She heard it, the sound of his shoes against the pavement behind her. She was not going to make it. She was going to snap and everything she worked for would be lost. Black Rose ran with everything she had to get away. Her mind was not clear enough for her to transport and her body was too shaken up to be able to take it.

Black Rose felt her hand slip into his and her arm yanked backwards. Her body jerked and her feet twisted under her. Her body was encircled by arms far stronger than she was at the moment. Black Rose's hand found his face and she pushed it away.

"Stop fighting me stupid! You're injured!" Jin cried angrily.

"Then release me!" Black Rose snapped ignoring her throbbing back, and the warmth of Jin's body. She felt Jin's arms move from around her and she stumbled forwards, surprised by the lack of pull against her. Her legs were shaking slightly and the pain came back in full force. Black Rose bit back a cry of pain and tried to walk forward but her legs would not allow her move.

"You're so stupid," Jin muttered angrily. "Your whole back is burned and you act as if you can just move so easily."

"Why are you getting so upset?" Black Rose snapped, standing up. "I don't see you injured."

Jin walked to Black Rose and before she could register it, his hands slid up her arms and squeezed her shoulders tenderly.

"I don't want to see you hurt," Jin snapped back, softly. "Doesn't that matter?"

Black Rose could not stop the warmth spreading throughout her. His hands were warm against her bare shoulders and his palms were light against her burns. She felt Jin's breath against her shoulder before it registered that his lips were gracing one of her burns.

A light feeling spread through her body at the softness of Jin's caress.

"Doesn't this matter?" Jin's question was barely heard through the loudness of Black Rose's heart.

"What is this?" Black Rose whispered, feeling herself fall into the warmth of Jin's body. She never realized how cold she was.

No. This was not right. She was just getting overwhelmed by the moment. She did not even like the way her heart was beating! It was all because he was worried about her. Who know if he was even being sincere? Whatever she was feeling, it needed to be crushed. Jin Tohari be cursed.

"Never touch me again," she growled before transporting to her house.

Winterwonderland

Jin stumbled out of bed with a big grin on his face. Today was the day of the school trip. He was ready to enjoy the day at Winterwonderland! Jin rolled his bag down the stairs and ran to the bathroom. He sang broken tunes as he washed. He felt refreshed and awake after his shower. After wiping away the steam that rested on the mirror, Jin began to fix his hair. He noticed a purplish mark on his abdomen and looked down at it. His fingers brushed over the mark and he realized it was a lot smaller than it had been a few weeks ago when he got it playing dodge ball. But it was still there, and that was what startled him.

He remembered walking home from school that day they played dodge ball. It was windy and the force of the wind was strong enough to blow a person over. Jin remembered the way Xia looked as she tried to move the hair out of her eyes during gym class. She was almost… pretty. Jin laughed.

"She *is* pretty," he said putting on his clothes. "Just a little violent."

Besides all of that, she was Black Rose. Even if she didn't admit it yet, Jin was positive Xia Chang was Black Rose. Jin would make her tell him. He just needed the right opportunity. The school trip might be the best shot he got. Jin walked out of the washroom ready to go to school. He passed the calendar and noticed that his parents would be coming home from their expedition after the weekend. That meant that he would go back to living in his own house. Jin's insides fluttered with excitement. With his parents home, he would be able to learn more about the outside world! Jin closed his eyes and sighed. Finally, he would get some more answers about the outside world.

Jin entered the kitchen and looked for some food. The bus ride to Winterwonderland would be about five hours. That would give him enough time to do some more research.

For the past few weeks Black Rose did more of her annoying escape tricks, but this time she had no intention of being cornered or spoken to. And to make Jin's life any more difficult she was more secretive than when he first met her. But finally by a stroke of luck, Jin had cornered her with every intention of getting Black Rose to talk. He was less than a foot away and he had reached out to grab her. Quicker than lightning though she pushed him away, jumped off the roof and disappeared into thin air. That had been the previous night.

"I was so close!" Jin growled as he poured himself a bowl of cereal. "If I don't catch her in the act, we'll never get anywhere!"

She sure moved well for a burn victim.

"Never go where Jin?" a small voice asked. Jin turned to face the doorway and saw his little sister looking at him with sleepy eyes. Her black hair fell into her face in a messy heap on her head. She had pink PJs on with blue ducks printed on the pants. Jin's eyes softened as he gazed at Aya Tohari.

"Come here, sweetie," Jin said and opened his arms to invite his sister to him. Aya padded over to Jin and lifted her arms to let Jin raise her.

"Where is Jin going?" Aya asked.

"Remember I said that I had a trip today?" Jin asked. "I'm going to be back in a few days."

"Is Uncle Tekeda going too?"
Jin shook his head.

"No, he'll be here to take care of you," Jin replied. "So you have to be a good girl and take care of him, okay?"
Aya nodded.

"Love, you Jin," she said. "You be good too."
Jin nodded.

"Of course," he said smiling. "Here, you finish this and then go back to sleep."
Aya nodded.

"See ya when you get back!" she said.

Jin kissed his little sister on her cheek and she giggled.

"Bye, tell uncle I said bye."

"Okies."

"Good girl," Jin said smiling. "Bye."

"Go already!"

Jin laughed and walked to the door. He put on his shoes and picked up his luggage and walked out the door. A wide grin spread across his face, as he met up with some people from his class on the way to school. They talked about what they were going to do and who they were going to room with. Soon they were at school and Jin's class was all ready to go. Class 1-A grouped together and talked loudly. Jin found one of his friends and talked with them animatedly.

"Jin, I have your picture ready," Erick Bastion said smiling. Erick was Jin's friend from kindergarten. He had dark skin and hair but amazingly light eyes. Erick wanted to be an artist and live his life creating works for rich patrons.

"Really, can I see it now?" Jin asked in excitement. Erick smirked.

"No."

Jin's smile faded from his face.

"Why not? Erick you said you'd have it ready last week! I can't keep waiting!" Jin growled angrily.

"You were fine then, you'll be fine now," Erick said grinning.

Jin stepped closer to Erick with a menacing look on his face.

"If you don't give me that picture now…!"

"You'll what?"

"Erick don't play with me! If I don't get the picture soon, I'm gonna go crazy!"

Erick laughed.

"Okay, I promise you'll get it at the end of the week."

Jin was about to jump Erick and shake him until he gave him his picture, when excited cries came from another group.

"Black Rose stopped those crimes! It was amazing!"

"Yeah! I heard about that!"

"She was really quick! I was there and I couldn't even see her properly!"

"You were really there? Tell us everything!"

Jin turned to listen. If they were talking about Black Rose, then he needed to hear all the information he could. Jin listened and looked at Erick, while he remained silent. Erick had his sketchpad out and had a pencil to it. He was furiously scribbling down little sketches of Black Rose from what the others were saying. Soon the conversation turned from Black Rose to dresses for the Winterwonderland ball. Jin looked around the crowd, no longer interested in the conversation.

He wanted to find her. His eyes scanned the edges of the courtyard and came upon what he was searching for.

Xia Chang was sitting on a bench reading a thick book. He could not see the title of the book or the author but it looked too intelligent for his tastes. Her light hair was tied in a messy bun at the top of her head. She wore a zippered navy hooded sweatshirt with a white collared shirt and dark jeans with white sneakers. Her black luggage was by her side. Jin grinned.

"I'll be right back," he said to Erick who nodded.

Jin walked over to Xia and sat beside her. Her face scrunched up in a disgusted manner that pleased Jin.

"Chang, how're you today? Ready to go?"

"Must you bother me so early in the morning?" Xia asked flipping a page.

Jin grinned at her back and said nothing. It was the best way to annoy Xia Chang. After seconds of silence, Jin decided to speak again. Silence was never really something he was good at.

"What're you reading?" he asked. Xia did not reply. Naturally. Jin reached over Xia and plucked her book away. She glared at him.

"What do you want?" she asked fiercely.

"To ask you a few questions about last night," Jin replied. He gave Xia's book a little toss as he spoke.

"What *about* last night?" Xia muttered angrily.

Jin grinned. She was not going to go down that easily.

"Where were you last night? I mean after the kidnapping incident," Jin asked.

Xia's eye visibly twitched. She was upset already.

"I was not *at* the kidnapping incident," Xia muttered. "I know where this is going so you can stop it!"

Jin leaned in and Xia stood up.

"What? Going already?" Jin asked following Xia as she started walking off.

"Get away from me," Xia said forcefully.

"If you knew where I was going with the conversation, you would also know that I have no intention of backing down," Jin said keeping up with every one of Xia's strides.

Xia sighed in frustration.

"Get away from me Tohari! I am in no mood to even be in your presence," She said in an 'I-can't-be-calm-now-but-I-am-trying-to-be' voice.

"But I'm very much in the mood to be in yours."

Xia whipped around, grabbed Jin by the collar and shoved him against the wall. Jin had not noticed until then that Xia had led him out of sight from all the teachers and students. Xia's expression was furious and dangerous and made Jin's heart picked up a beat.

"I'll tell you this one more time," Xia's voice was calm and cool but her expression betrayed her. "Stay away from me!"

Xia backed away from Jin, letting go of him, picked up her bags and left. Jin's eyes were wide and he was breathing again.

Did she scare him?

Her look just then… It seemed more than what a fifteen-year-old girl was capable of. Jin's heart started to beat at an irregular pace. She was exhilarating! Jin slowly got off the wall and dusted his backside off. He looked at his hands. They were shaking. A grin broke out on his face.

Cool, calm and always collected Xia Chang had lost control. That was why he was shaking. He made her finally lose it. She was crazy if she thought he was going to leave her alone now.

*   *   *

Hainai High School class 1-A arrived at Winterwonderland in the late afternoon and was promptly shown around on a tour. They would be able to go to the mountains the next day and the Winterwonderland Ball would be held the next evening. The third day was a free day to do whatever they pleased and Jin was looking forward to hitting the hot springs. The last day was a 'pack-your-bags' day and head back in the afternoon.

After the tour was finished the students of Hainai High had to settle into the rooms and get ready for dinner. Jin shared a room with Erick.

"So what'd you find out? Anything?" Erick asked as he sat on his bed sketching. Jin grinned.

"She's crazy," Jin said. "But that makes the chase that much better."

"Obsessed."

Jin's cheeks turned slightly pink and he glared.

"I am not! You'd want to know who saved your five-year-old sister too!"

Erick chortled.

"Give me that picture Erick! I don't know what I'm gonna do without it! Gimme a break, man! You *know* you can't get her out of your head!" Erick mimicked Jin. "You eat, sleep and breathe Black Rose. I hope I never become someone you chase."

Jin didn't mind being embarrassed, but being embarrassed by Erick Bastion was something completely different.

"Shut-up!" Jin said tossing his shirt at Erick. "I can't help it if I'm interested in her! I like to crack mysteries and she's the toughest one of all."

Erick Bastion's face cracked up and he started laughing hysterically.

"Toughest one of all...? You- you should maket those lines!" Erick said in between fits of laughter. Jin growled and walked into the bathroom, slamming the door shut.

Jin arrived at dinner wearing a black collared shirt and khakis. His hair was spiky- but it came that way. The just-rolled-out-of-bed hairstyle was one hundred percent natural. Jin sat at a table by the window and waited for more people to show up. The dinning area was large and screamed wealth. It had chandeliers of gold and crystal and floors of marble. The teachers were not joking when they said to dress nicely.

Some girls walked over to his table smiling and talking. Jin made light conversation and smiled. Soon after, the girls left Jin for their own table, Erick walked into the dining area wearing a lavender collared shirt with a yellow sweater tied around his neck and khakis. He looked around for a second before noticing Jin and walked over to him.

"They said that we had to dress nicely," he said as he sat down. "And I see why, this place is pretty ritzy."
Jin nodded.

"Yeah, I know," he said. "I wonder what they'll serve us."
Erick grinned.

"We're 'children', so we won't be getting the expensive stuff," he replied.

Jin nodded and flicked his glass. It made a ringing sound.

"You're used to this kind of stuff aren't you?" he asked Erick. "Your family's pretty high up right?"
Erick nodded.

"Even if I am, they want to disown me because I want to be an artist rather than some public figure."

"At least they-"

Jin's words were cut short as he looked up at the doorway. Erick grinned and turned his attention toward the entrance as well. It was as he had suspected. Black Rose, or rather, Xia Chang entered the room. Jin watched as she walked to her table and sat down. She was wearing a knee-length black velvet dress with a small bow tied around her midsection. Most of her hair cascaded down her back, but a little was tied in a braid. She really *was* pretty! Jin turned back around grinning. Erick rolled his eyes but was chuckling.

"*Obsessed,*" Erick said in singsong tones.
Jin, who was in a daze, snapped out of it and glared.

"I am not!" Jin muttered. "I can't help it if she looks like Black Rose right now!"

"So you *are* more interested in Black Rose than just finding out her identity," Erick said. "I knew it."

"You don't know anything!" Jin snapped.

Erick Bastion grinned. A few more people walked over to Jin's table and sat down. Minutes later the dinner started. He hated being embarrassed in front of his friends so he would not admit it to them, but all night he watched Xia Chang. What would she give away to him about her being Black Rose? She dressed in black tonight, nothing to go on there besides the fact Black Rose always wore black. She did not smile, she never smiled but she did eat politely. Okay so she had manners. That was nice to know. Giving up for a minute, he watched a few of his classmates dance after dinner.

Jin sighed as he walked back to his room. Tomorrow evening would be the Winterwonderland Ball and it would be the highlight of the entire trip for many people. Jin was hoping something exciting would happen; preferably Black Rose showing up so he could confront her again, but he did not want to get his hopes up. Jin slid the key card into the slot and opened his door when the blue light blinked. He had half a mind to lock it and let Erick fend for himself for the night, but he needed that sketch his friend kept talking about at dinner.

Unfortunately if Jin locked him out, there would be no picture waiting for him at the end of the trip and he needed this last sketch to make a complete picture of Black Rose. Jin closed the door behind him and rested his head on it. He closed hit eyes and sighed.

She looked so pretty. Jin thought, as he ran his fingers through his midnight hair. *What makes you tick Black Rose? What makes me want to chase you so much?*

Jin chuckled darkly. It did not matter why he wanted to get her. As long as he did.

"Keep running Black Rose… one day I will catch you."

Unmasked!

"Woo!" Jin yelled as he flew off a bump faster than was safe. He twisted his body and did a 360 degree turn in the air, before landing. Continuing down the slope, Jin hit every bump in the snow that was available to him. He was not amazing at snowboarding, but he was willing to give everything a try. If it meant falling on his face, it meant falling on his face. But at least he attempted it once. Jin safely made it to the bottom falling only four in the process.

"Alright! That was great!" Jin cried. Erick suddenly flew past him and came to a fast halt.

Arrogant little...! Jin thought bitterly.

"You didn't look like a complete idiot out there! I'm proud!" Erick said grinning. Jin growled and lunged forward trapping his best friend in a headlock.

"Shut-up you annoying little know-it-all!" he yelled yanking at his head. "Not all of us do this every year!"
Erick tried to move away but was unsuccessful.

"Ow, Jin that hurts!" he cried trying to break free of Jin's hold. "Okay! Okay I get your point!"

"Is that Chang?!"

"What's she doing?!"

"Look Tohari! It's Chang!"

Jin immediately let go of Erick and looked toward the mountain. Xia Chang was zooming down the mountain looking "Awesome!" as Jin's classmates shouted in awe. Jin felt a pang of envy. Was everyone better than he was? No! He was not going to take that! Xia jumped off the ramp and flipped backwards expertly. Her hair whipped out behind her like a flag in the wind. Her black clothes made her stand out even more, which was ironic. Black Rose stood in the shadows while Xia, even if it was against her consciousness, stood out like a sore thumb.

"She's good…" Erick said watching the girl jump off another bump. "Better than you are."

"I can see that!" Jin snapped. But he did not really care. A grin spread across his face.

"What other things do you know, Black Rose?"

"Oh boy," Erick muttered. "Jin, can you just have fun? Without thinking about Black Rose for a moment?"

Jin did not hear his friend because he was too busy staring as Xia stopped a few feet in front of them. Before he could even question her, throngs of students came up to her asking her where she learned all of her stunts. Jin grumbled and dragged Erick away from the crowd. He would talk to Xia later. It would be better if no one else were in the way.

Jin and Erick slid down the slopes until afternoon. They had to get ready for the Winterwonderland Ball that was to take place in the evening. Talking loudly, Jin led the way to the room and opened it. Erick took the washroom first and Jin looked for the suit he was planning on wearing. The teachers said that the theme of the Ball was a secret. Jin wondered what it was and if he was dressing accordingly. He wanted to have fun, but he wanted to work more. He needed to have Xia confirm that she was Black Rose! But what then? What would he do after that? If she did say she was Black Rose, what *could* he do after that?

"Why am I chasing after her in the first place?" Jin asked himself. He placed his white bowtie on the bed and fingered the collar of his suit. The gold pinstripe was a subtle, but an inviting touch to Jin's suit. Jin's mind slowly took him away by the rhythm of the languid stroke of his fingers.

The lights were gentle but bright. The music flowed through the room caressing the hearts of the couples dancing. Jin walked down the staircase with a grin on his face. His smile was for one girl only. Jin walked over to the fair-haired beauty, ignoring the sighs and whispers around him. She was wearing a flowing pale pink dress and a gold necklace and looked beautiful. He offered her a flower. She took it with hesitation.

"You don't have to hide it anymore, Xia. I know you are Black Rose," Jin said in a smooth voice.

"But you aren't supposed to know!" Xia said looking away. "How'd you find out?"

"I'm Jin Tohari, ace detective! I had to find out," Jin said. "You couldn't fool me for long."

"Jin... I can't-"

Jin lifted his finger to Xia's lips to silence her. He plucked the flower out of her slender fingers and placed it in her hair.

"Shh," he whispered, "we'll work it out. But dance with me now."

Xia had a faint smile to her face.

"Oh Jin..." Xia said blushing.

Jin placed one hand on Xia's hip and the other in her own hand. She placed her free hand on his shoulder. Jin led her in a waltz.

"Xia," he whispered to her tenderly.

"Jin..." her soft voice sighed.

"Xia..."

"Jin...."

"Xia..."

"Yo *Jin*!"

Jin Tohari jumped from his daydream, looking around wildly.

"Hu?"

Erick sighed.

"You were dreaming man," he said. "No Black Roses in here."

Jin's gaze slowly reached his best friend and realization settled in.

"Oh geez," he muttered slapping his hand to his forehead. "Forget everything you heard!"

Erick Bastion grinned.

"Oh yeah, *sure*," he said mockingly. "*We'll work it out but dance with me now.*" Erick started laughing and waltzing around the room. Jin hated him so much as he flushed and ran into the washroom. Best friends were overrated.

All the boys of Hainai High, fully dressed and suited, had to meet up in one room. The male teachers walked in soon after, carrying boxes. Jin was curious to know what the theme was going to be. He was still hoping something big would happen so that Black Rose would be forced to show up. Mr. A placed the last box down and grinned.

"Gentlemen, you look acceptable," he said grinning. "I bet you've all been wondering what the theme of the Winter-wonderland Ball will be, this evening. Well, you don't have to wait any longer."

Jin was on the balls of his feet in anticipation. Jungle theme? Marine theme? *Ancient Civilizations*? No, maybe that one was over the top.

"The theme of the evening is..." Mr. A opened the box in front of him and masks peeked out from the edges, "a masquerade!"

An excited buzz filled the air. Jin grinned widely. How perfect! A masquerade was the perfect setting for a chase.

"We're glad you're excited about it," Joe Kane said. "Now get in a line so we can properly match your mask with your suits."

Jin got in line, anxious. When he got to the front, Joe Kane gave him a black mask lined with gold. It covered his eyes and nose elegantly.

"Have fun," Joe smiled. "*Please* have fun. No rivalries with Chang tonight, okay?"

"I can't promise that Kane," Jin said grinning.

Jin laughed and exited the room. This could be the chance he was looking for! Jin walked to the ballroom while he put on his mask. This was going to be the night! Black

Rose was going to be caught, whether she wanted to be or not.

Jin walked into a room filled with masks and colors. Girls were in pretty flowing dresses adorned with masks that fitted their pictures perfectly. Boys wore suits with masks covering their eyes mysteriously. The room was very large with walls molded into beautiful columns of painted gold and pearl. The windows were large and looked out to a beautiful starry night sky. Large windowed doors led the way to the balconies. It was the perfect place for a masquerade.

The music was lively and many people were enjoying it. Dinner was lined along a wall; ready to be eaten at any time. Everything seemed almost unreal. Jin found a few people standing by the walls and got them to dance. There was no reason to be standing there bored! Jin laughed as he danced around the ballroom enjoying his time, but something caught his eye and his heart quickened a beat.

She wore a cropped satin black dress that made her pale skin look as if it were glowing. A white ribbon crossed her midsection, forming a bow around her back. It made her whole thing come together. And Jin found his eyes trailing along the long line of her exposed back.

Xia Chang was walking around the room slowly with her black and white mask tied around her head of fair curls.

Jin grinned and exited the dance floor in her direction. She seemed to notice him and weaved her way into the mass of happy people. He lost her in the crowd and smirked. If she wanted to play a game, then by all means he would play. Jin slowly walked around the room following the little hints she left behind her. The trim of her black gown, the tips of her light hair, her silhouette. The chase was all the more interesting when there was work involved.

Jin could not remember a time when his heart was beating as fast as it was at this moment.

He noticed that Xia stopped walking. He looked past her to see that a teacher stopped her to speak with her. Jin walked closer taking the opportunity. He noticed that a door to a balcony was open. *Perfect.* As soon as the teacher turned away, Jin grabbed his chase's wrist and offered her a smirk. Xia did not even have the time to look behind her to see if the self-proclaimed detective had ceased following her.

"Dance with me," Jin said. He pulled Xia towards the open doors and placed one hand on her waist and the other in hers. Jin noticed that her dress had rose prints lightly in the fabric. He led the waltz without a second's hesitation and Xia had to cooperate or face getting her toes stepped on. She glared angrily up at Jin.

"What are you scheming?" Xia seethed.

"I don't scheme, I plan," Jin replied. "But I'll tell you, if you dance with me for a while."

Xia glared angrily. Waltzing couples floated past before she started speaking again.

"You really *are* annoying," she said moving Jin's hand to the proper spot on her back. "And I had half a mind to give you some credit."
Jin nodded.

"It's a gift," he said softly. "You seem to have many yourself. Beauty must be one of them."

"Stop talking," Xia snapped, "and flattery will not work on me! What do you hope to gain by this?"

Jin grinned, twirled Xia and pulled her right back into his arms.

"What do I hope to gain?" Jin repeated. "I plan on taking that pretty black mask off your face… and exposing the real you."

Xia's grip on Jin's shoulder became tight. Jin's masked face brightened with interest.

"Just *try* and take it off," Xia whispered tauntingly, "I dare you Jin Tohari, *master* detective."
Jin chuckled and pulled Xia a little closer.

"I'll make sure to catch you tonight," Jin softly whispered close to Xia's ear, "…Black Rose."

Xia tensed up but when Jin twirled her again it was surprisingly fluid.

"And *I'll* make sure I never get caught," Xia lifted herself close enough to Jin's face to whisper. Jin felt his cheek turn slightly red. He was not used to being so intimate with Xia, but he was quickly adjusting.

Xia held a faint smirk on her face before moving further away from Jin. He had to admit, Xia was a bit like him when he thought about it. She was equally stubborn and unrelenting.

Jin led Xia around the balcony for another minute until the waltz's fluid tune was noticeably about to end. Xia moved to get away from Jin, but he gripped her tighter and pulled her even closer.

"It's rude to give up in the middle of a dance," Jin said sparing the angry girl a wink.

"I would rather give up than endure this any longer."

Jin chuckled.

"Why?" he questioned. "Are you so anxious to relinquish your mask to me?"

Xia's pretty mask could not hide loathing in her eyes.

"Big words don't suit you and my mask, Jin Tohari, will never be relinquished to you."

Jin smiled slyly. He gave Xia one last twirl before holding her tightly.

"Don't be so sure, Chang. I think I might be the one on top."

The waltz ended and Jin released Xia from her captivity. She rushed off the balcony and Jin knew she was absolutely furious. Jin laughed again.

"That was great," he said.

"I'm glad you're having fun torturing poor Chang."

Jin turned his head to the side. Erick walked onto the balcony.

"I wasn't *torturing* her necessarily," Jin started, "…what am I saying? Of course I was! And I did enjoy it, thank-you very much."

Erick shook his head.

"Well don't tell Kane that," Erick said. "He's practically shaking with joy over at the teacher's table… Something about you and Chang finally getting along. Obviously he missed the way she left."

Jin laughed loudly.

"Well we can't make them all happy," he said. The Winterwonderland ball was indeed something he was enjoying.

*   *   *

"This is the life…" Jin sighed.

It was the last day before they were going to leave for home and Jin made a decision to enjoy the hot springs. After a hard day of falling and competing with Xia Chang, Jin thought he deserved a rest.

"…That yard sale was killer…" Jin groaned and let the water relax his sore body.

"But I bet you're happy you caught Chang in the middle of it and you both tumbled down the hill together," Erick said, squeezing the water out of the washcloth onto his head.

"Yeah… that was great," Jin sighed. "She wasn't too happy but it was worth it."

"She hit you pretty hard though. Sure you won't bruise?" Erick asked between his laughter.

"Of *course* I'm going to bruise!" Jin cried rubbing his cheek. "She hits way too hard for a girl! But while bruises go away, the picture of her shocked face will lie with me forever."

"Obsessed."

Jin was about to reply, when screams were heard from the girl's side of the springs. Jin shared a confused look with his best friend before he heard cries for help. Jin shot out of the water and as quickly as he could, threw on some clothes and rushed to the other side.

Luck was on his side and the girls seemed to be wearing some form of clothing. Jin rushed to one of the girls to ask what was going on.

"E-Emmi s-she's gonna drown!" the girl said through her tears. Jin's eyes widened and he rushed to the spring. He was wondering why no one was going to rescue her and when he reached the hot spring he received his answer. The girl, Emmi Gordon, was caught between a rock and the large opening the water was going into.

"Someone get a teacher!" Jin heard Erick yell. Jin was confused as to how Emmi got to where she was in the first place. The man-made hot springs were supposed to be safe. Jin jumped into the spring and instantly found out.

Instead of the water pushing outward, it was pulling inwards toward the opening. Inside the opening Jin knew there was a fan large enough to slice Emmi up. But…

Jin took hold of the edge of the spring and started slowly towards the unconscious girl. Jin's body suddenly jerked toward the opening and a few girls cried out to him. Jin grasped the edge tighter. The pull was far stronger than he was. Jin stared at the unconscious girl, lost for an answer.

Suddenly Jin heard gasping and a few seconds later, he saw black boots land on the rock that kept Emmi from entering the fan's wrath. Jin looked up slightly surprised. Black Rose knelt down to pull Emmi out of the water. The girls on the side cheered loudly.

Jin rushed out of the hot spring.

"Bring her over here!" Jin called to Black Rose.
A shutter from the spring made Black Rose almost loose balance.

"Black Rose! Are you alright?" Jin asked on edge. For some reason, his adrenaline was starting to pump. Black Rose steadied herself and jumped over to Jin's side. She stumbled slightly because of the extra weight and Jin caught her.

"You alright?" he asked.

Black Rose nodded and placed Emmi Gordon down on the ground. Jin immediately started to remove the water from her lungs. As soon as Emmi spluttered, coughed and breathed, the self-proclaimed detective sighed in relief, but he was not completely worried. Black Rose was close by anyway.

Jin took off his shirt and placed it under the semi-conscious girl's head. He heard footsteps and looked up to see the teacher rush down to tend to Emmi. The rescued girl was too tired to do anything, but smile faintly.

A tingle in the back of his mind made Jin's head snap up. Black Rose was not there. *That little sneak!* Jin thought as he smirked. From the corner of his eye, Jin saw her slip into the building, unnoticed by everyone except for him. He was suddenly very exhilarated and hastily followed Black Rose into the hotel. Within seconds, Black Rose noticed Jin and broke out running down an empty corridor.

Jin ran faster to catch up to Black Rose. He grabbed her by the hand and yanked her to him. A jolt of excitement ran through his veins at her touch. Black Rose struggled to break free of Jin's hold.

"I'm not- *not* letting you go until I have your mask off!" Jin growled, as he fought to keep Black Rose's fingers from clawing his eyes out.

"What is the point if you already know who I am?" Black Rose cried. "Curse you Tohari! *Get off me!*"

Jin slammed Black Rose against the wall in his effort to keep her from escaping.

"If you know that I know, why are you fighting so much?!" Jin yelled back. He dodged Black Rose's fingernails by centimeters. "*You almost made me blind!* Black Rose- Chang- watch those cat-claws of yours!"

"I cannot allow you to get any closer that is why I am fighting! Why are you so persistent?! Get off of me Tohari!" Black Rose shouted back. She put her whole body into resisting Jin. She did not want to be unmasked. The consequences were too much for her to handle.

"No!"

"Why are you trying so hard?!"

"So I can see the truth with-*stop it*- with my own eyes!!"

Jin was struggling to keep a hold on Black Rose while trying to tire her out, but the opposite was happening.

"Is that it?!" Black Rose cried. "Is *that* why you have been chasing me relentlessly?! *If you do not stop this...!*"

Jin could tell she was getting worn out. Her breathing was labored but at the same time, he was becoming tired as well.

"No! But I don't know what else there is!" Jin fought to reach for Black Rose's mask. She lunged away from Jin causing Jin to loose balance. Jin fell on top of her but with one smooth movement she pinned him to the floor. Jin was in a state of shock. His breathin was heavy. Black Rose was also panting.

"Who is on top now?" she taunted. Jin smirked

"Me."

Jin lunged forward to reach Black Rose's face and yanked at the mask. It ripped off with a snap. A bright light burst from Xia and settled down to gentle sparkles. Xia Chang scrambled off Jin looking at him with terrified eyes.

Andez

"What did... what did you just do?!" Xia spluttered looking lost. Something about her seemed so fragile. Jin thought she would break in a second by the way her face looked. In a flash, Xia stumbled to her feet and bolted down the hallway. Jin hopped up and charged after her. Xia's steps were unsteady and she looked about ready to collapse right then and there, but she did not stop running. She made it all too easy for Jin to catch up to her.

"Don't touch me!" Xia cried as Jin held her wrist again.

"What's the point of you running away now Xia? I already knew the truth," Jin said softly. The unmasked Black Rose stumbled over her feet, successfully slumping to the floor and slipping out of Jin's grasp.

"You do not know what is going to happen! I hate you Tohari!"

Jin gently padded to the front of Xia and kneeled down. He reached for her hand. She snatched her arm away.

"Do not think you are familiar with me because of this! I will not tolerate it!"

Jin cocked an eyebrow.

"What will you tolerate then?" he asked.

Xia's hands balled into fists.

"You embarrass me, then mock me? I cannot bare the shame that has...!"

Xia's cheeks were pink with anger but she did not say anything else.

"We can try to work something out..." Jin said. "This isn't that bad."

"You do not know anything!" Xia yelled.

"Then tell me what I don't know!" Jin shouted back. "I already know your biggest secret for all I'm concerned and I don't plan on leaving you alone now! So either get used to me or get rid of me."

Xia glared vehemently.

"Who are you to give me commands?"

"The boy who found out your secret. Now tell me that you aren't in a compromising position right now."

"What do you hope to gain by this? My humiliation?" Jin looked at Xia before looking away.

"You wouldn't believe me if I told you what I wanted to gain."

Xia scoffed.

"You chase me for weeks and don't even know why you are doing it? Some self-proclaimed detective you are."

"At least I wasn't clumsy enough to get my identity figured out by that self-proclaimed detective!"

Jin and Xia glared at each other for a long moment.

"We have to come up with some sort of agreement or you will not be leaving this floor anytime soon," Jin said in a serious voice.

Xia glared but looked defeated.

"I'm not sure you have many choices…either come with me or be killed. I would prefer if you chose the second option," Xia said. Jin noticed, with a bit of displeasure, that Xia's unemotional mask was placed firmly back on her face. He liked it better with her feelings out a little more.

"I think the first option is the one I'm choosing," Jin said grinning. "What do you mean anyway?"

Xia looked like she much rather not explain, but she did not have a choice.

"You will have to appeal to my parents and I will have to explain what has happened." Xia said. "We need to talk about this some other time. We have to get back."

"You look really tired," he muttered, "are you alright?"

Xia did not reply and stood up. She stumbled a little and Jin moved to steady her. His hands landed on her waist and elbow.

"Geez, are you alright? You seem really tired," Jin asked concerned.

Xia wiggled her way out of Jin's grasp and started down the hall back to the rooms. She did not reply. Jin shrugged and walked after her. A grin was on his face. He wondered what would happen now that Black Rose knew she was no longer a secret. He felt accomplished, but not fulfilled, now that he had finally caught Black Rose. Jin looked at Xia trying to be strong and walking as fast as humanly possible. It was sad that she thought she had to be the woman with the strongest will in Hainai.

*   *   *

Tekeda Tohari's two-story brick mansion welcomed Jin back with open arms. It seemed very cozy now that he looked at it, but it was not as comfortable as his own home. Jin walked into his uncle's house with a grin on his face. He heard voices coming from the sitting room. Jin smirked and set down his luggage. He started taking off his shoes when his little sister's head popped from behind the doorway. A huge grin spread across her face.

"Jin!" Aya Tohari squealed as she ran towards Jin. Her arms were spread as wide as her smile and she rammed into Jin. Jin winced but laughed it off. He picked up his little sister, kissing her on her cheeks.

"Were you a good girl?" he asked hugging his sister then letting her down.

Aya nodded and her raven curls bounced happily. Jin took off his remaining shoe and walked into the hallway. He lifted Aya up again and spun her around. She giggled happily.

"Piggyback ride!" Aya squealed. Jin laughed and lifted Aya Tohari to his back.

"Ready?" he asked.

"Go, piggy go!" she laughed. Jin nodded and hobbled around the foyer with Aya in his back. He galloped into the sitting room, spun around and plopped Aya onto a couch.

Then he proceeded to tickle her mercilessly. Giggles and squeals filled the room.

"I see Aya's back to normal."

Jin turned around smiling at Toi Tohari, his father. He had long brown hair that flowed down his back. His features were strikingly handsome and youthful. He had dark green eyes that were always playful yet burdened. Jin could never figure out what troubled his father because his personality only showed nonchalance.

Jin kissed his sister on her forehead before going to his father and mother.

"I've missed you," Jin said hugging his father.

"We know" Are Tohari said softly. "Your sister has been moody all day." She placed a hand on her son's cheek and embraced him fondly. Are Tohari had long, dark hair for as long as Jin could remember. She always wore it down, like her husband. Her cheerful and sometimes childish behavior made Jin wonder why she wanted to have children, since she was such a big child herself. Still, she had a look to her that made people look more than once. Her beauty was often times breathtaking. Her husband was lucky.

"Mom," Jin said smiling, "you're embarrassing me."
Toi and Are Tohari smiled.

"Let me tell you about the site we went to!" Are said excitedly. Toi winked at Jin and placed an arm around his wife's back while she spoke. Aya sat in Jin's lap while their mother started explaining.

"It used to be a temple to a people long since dead," Are started "and forgotten."

"The Eracium?" Jin asked.

"Yes," Are replied. "The Eracium Radicals. But this is strictly Tohari house information, okay? You know the routine."
Jin and Aya nodded.

"Great, well this temple was not high temple, no it looked more like a… what's the way to say it, honey?" Are asked her husband.

"A *parkitsta*," Toi replied. "A village temple."

"Is that some sort of outer world language?" Jin asked.

"Yes, but it isn't used anymore… well it *is* used but that is an entirely different story," Are replied. "Now this *parkitsta* had a few hidden rooms in it. And I have to tell you, it is a wonder we even found the place!"

"Why?" Jin asked.

Are smiled.

"Because for the past, I don't know, *thirty* years there has been a desert storm covering the area. Just as Toi and I were around there it seemed to have ceased."

"Just like that?" Jin asked suspiciously.

"No, not just like that," Toi amended. "You know how your mother likes to over exaggerate things."

"I do not exaggerate things!" Are said hitting Toi playfully. "What I meant is that we had to wait a few days for the storm to calm down. But as we were there, it generally slowed until it disappeared all together. It was amazing."

"Was it some sort of outside world magic?" Jin asked interested.

Are and Toi shrugged.

"We can't be certain… but we found some very interesting information at the site."

Jin's eyes opened wide.

"Like what?" he asked scooting closer.

"A story about two lovers," Are replied dreamily. "And something else."

"Something else?"

"Yes," Are smiled. "A prophecy for future lovers."

Jin hummed and looked to the side. He looked thoughtful for a moment.

"…Does the prophecy have anything to do with the…. Organizations?" Jin asked.

Toi raised his eyebrows.

"Sure… but be careful who you talk about the Organizations to," he replied.

Jin nodded.

"Of course! I don't talk about it to anyone other than you guys… you know that," Jin said. "No one else really understands."

Toi and Are nodded.

"Naturally," Toi said, "the people here are afraid of the outside world. Are and I just don't fit in."

Jin shook his head.

"Don't say that! You and mom are really nice people! Besides, what about those people you keep sphereing?" Jin asked.

Are laughed.

"Oh, they don't fit in either! We're the perfect friends!" Are said smiling. "Back to our work, Toi and I are trying to decipher the messages in the temple. We brought back some samples so it will go better than expected."

Jin raised an eyebrow.

"Are you supposed to take *samples* from work?" he asked.

Are shook her head.

"No, but we discovered it- so technically we own it. As you know Jin, we are not part of a group," Are said. "And rules are a little different out there."

Jin nodded.

"So you own the rights to the site?" he asked.

Are looked at Toi. Toi shrugged.

"Well, you know that the outside world is in war right now right between the Organizations?" Are asked.

"Yeah…you've mentioned it," Jin replied. "What? So they fight over sites or something?"

"Or something," Toi replied. "It all depends on who owns the site."

Jin's eyes widened.

"So are you guys in the war or something? Did you get dragged in as well?" Jin asked worriedly.

Are smiled.

"You don't have to worry about us, Jin," Are said. "We have owned sites for years now. Really, you don't have to worry about us."

Jin nodded but was still worried about his parents. What if something happened to them while they were in the war? What if they were going to be taken hostage and killed?

"But… it is a war right? You could get killed," Jin said feeling panicked.

"It isn't the type of war you're thinking about, Jin." Are said. "We're not on a battlefield or anything, so we won't be killed."

Jin still frowned. He jumped when Toi laughed.

"You really have a sour face Jin," his father said. "Please, don't worry about us. We will be fine."

Jin was still uncertain but nodded.

"Why don't you take your sister to bed and then go yourself? It's pretty late," Toi said. Jin looked down to find Aya curled up in his lap, sleeping peacefully.

"Goodnight, mom, dad," Jin said carefully standing up. He rested Aya on his shoulder and smiled.

"Night honey," Are said softly. She kissed Aya on her cheek and Jin on his head. "Have a nice rest."

Jin's eyes flickered crimson.

"I always do, *kohnah*."

Are's eyes softened.

"Good," she said quietly.

"Goodnight *kanti*."

Jin looked over to his father with a soft smile planted on his face. His eyes glowed slightly.

"*Kohvah*," Jin's voice was soft and deep.

Are gave Aya and Jin one last hug before pushing them off to bed. She called to them goodnights before going back to the living room. She placed herself on her husband's armrest and rested her head on his shoulder. Toi wrapped his arm around his wife's waist and pulled her until she was sitting in his lap.

"You didn't have to talk to Cayn like that…" Toi said softly. "You might get him riled."
Are giggled and snuggled closer.

"It seems he's finally accepted you as his *father*," Are said.
Toi nodded.

"Yes," he said. "I'm glad."

"I'm glad you're glad… what do you suppose is his reason for contacting us?"
Toi shrugged.

"I suppose it is almost time."
Are laughed.

"One big happy family," she started, "all over again."
Toi hugged his wife close.

"Jin's grown so much," he said in a quiet voice.
Are nodded.

"I'm happy…and sad."
Toi gently stroked his wife's soft hair.

"I love you."
Are laughed.

"I know."

Training Day

It was early in the morning when Jin decided to get out of his bed and do his daily exercise. His nerves would not rest and staying in bed any longer seemed to give him no rest. Today was the day Xia had told him her parent's were available. Jin had to win over their trust in order to gain the rights to work with her as Black Rose's partner.

"Alright Jin! I can do this," Jin said to himself after washing his face. He grinned and made his way to the kitchen to salvage some food for his breakfast.

Jin looked up at the large mansion and whistled. The Chang residence was nicer than he expected. It was not nearly as cold as he imagined it. The front walkway was made of stone, which led to a beautiful Tudor styled mansion. The front yard was large with tall trees placed on the sides of the path, shading it from the sun. During warmer days it would prove to be a very comfortable place to walk down. Hedges lined the property in a grand display of roses. Jin walked down the walkway, slightly nervous.

"Okay, so Black Rose- I mean Chang has a little money... Nothing to worry about..." Jin told himself. "You're fine... *fine.*"

The self-proclaimed detective wore a pair of dark jeans with a black long-sleeve shirt. He looked presentable. It was a weekend and he was a teenager. He was about to meet parents, but he did not look like a bum. Jin breathed several deep breaths to calm his nerves. He had not been this nervous in a while. He was nervous because he was about to meet people who let their child run around the city doing older-than-should-be things, wearing a costume like it was okay. It *was* okay, but as soon as Jin knocked on the door he started wondering who these people really were.

Xia opened the door. She looked like she would rather not be polite but her parents were right behind her.

"Come in," Xia said politely.

"Thanks," Jin walked in and took note of the foyer. It was spacious and handsomely decorated. It was a combination of feminine and masculine tastes that warmly welcomed guests into the house.

"*Quelpi* do introduce us to your *friend*," a beautiful woman caught Jin's gaze. She was softly spoken and polite, had pretty light hair, light blue eyes and a kind but motherly expression on her face. She did not seem like the type of woman to go down with out a fight. That is, until her husband said something.

"Yes love, what is his name?" Jin's head turned to the man speaking and realized why Xia turned out to be so attractive. Her father was tall and darker than her mother, his hair was shoulder length, black, and his eyes were dark brown. He had a demanding sort of feel around him and Jin did not want to do anything that made him upset.

A long, thin scar marked his face, stretching from his left eyebrow across the bridge of his nose.

"*Fadi*, *mothi*, this is Jin Tohari, Tohari *fadi*, *mothi*," Xia said in a why-am-I-bothering tone of voice. Jin had no idea what *fadi* or *mothi* meant but smiled like he did.

"Nice to meet you," he said, "and you have a lovely home."

Xia's parents nodded. Xia's father walked over to Jin, took his hand and kissed both of his cheeks. Jin flushed as the man backed away and Xia's mother did the same thing. Jin's face was as red as a tomato and he was confused.

"Please, call me Neisei and my wife you may call Tudios. It really is an honor to meet the young man that has unmasked Black Rose." Xia's father said grinning.

Jin's eyes widened, his embarrassment forgotten.

"You're not mad about that?" he asked surprised and relieved.

Tudios smiled warmly.

"Not at all," she said. "Our *quelpi* was getting overly confident and I think this will humble her some. Please, come into the sitting room. I'll serve tea."

Jin nodded and followed Neisei and Xia into the sitting room. *Maybe this won't be so bad after all,* Jin mused.

"So, tell me about yourself," Neisei said in his low voice.

Jin laughed a little nervously.

"I'm in Xia's grade, same age...um..."

Jin had no idea what to say, or what to do. Normally he would have no problem telling people who he was, but this time he was nervous.

"Don't be nervous around us Tohari-*kai*," Neisei started, "because I assure you, we will not be nervous around you."

Jin smiled, relieved but still could not figure out what to say. His eyes darted to Xia. She was looking away.

"Do you have any siblings?" Neisei asked.

"Yes, I have a little sister, Aya. She's five," Jin replied. "I'm the only boy but mom and dad have been talking about another child. I'm not sure if they're being serious or not."

Neisei chuckled. Jin saw something in his eyes that made him think that Neisei knew all about his parent's antics. *But that can't be true. We've only just met,* Jin thought.

"Do you like what your parents do Tohari-*kai*?" Tudios Chang walked into the room carrying a tray of tea and sweets. Xia immediately stood up and started unloading the tray. She placed a cup of tea in front of her father and then one in front of Jin.

"My parents are archaeologists, so I think their work it very interesting. But lately I think that it is getting pretty dangerous," Jin replied. He took a sip of his tea and noticed it was sweet. Taking in some more, he smiled. A wave of nostalgia washed over Jin making him sigh. He had no idea why he felt so homesick when his home was only a fifteen-minute walk away.

"How do you like it?" Tudios asked. "Is the flavor too strong?"

Jin smiled warmly at Tudios.

"It is very good," he replied. "Not strong at all."

Tudios smiled and passed the plate of cookies to Jin.

"I'm glad you enjoy it. Do you believe your mother and father would take a liking to it as well?'

Jin gasped.

"I'm sorry! I forgot to tell you dad and mom were coming!" Jin said quickly.

Neisei chuckled.

"Don't worry. We thought as much," he said, lifting his teacup to his lips. There was a knock on the door and Neisei grinned.

"See? Your parents are already here. *Quelpi*, please answer the door. *Bavdnah* please prepare more tea."

Xia got up and went to the door while Tudios went in the direction of the kitchen. Neisei stood up and Jin quickly followed. In a few seconds, Jin heard his mother and father's voices, then they appeared in the sitting room. Jin smiled at his parents and waved slightly. Neisei walked over to Toi and took his hand, kissing both cheeks. *It has to be some sort of custom,* Jin thought, remembering how Neisei and Tudios did the same thing to him. Neisei walked over to Are and took her hand. He kissed her cheeks and they laughed together like old friends. Toi was carrying the tray of tea and placed it on the table. He turned to Tudios, took her hand, and then kissed her cheeks.

The interactions between the parents confused Jin. He looked up at Xia and could tell she noticed something as well. His parents and her parents were acting as if they were best friends.

"Please sit down," Neisei said smiling. Toi and Are sat next to Jin and Xia moved to sit beside her parents.

"Thank-you for having us," Toi said smiling. He flicked his long hair behind his shoulder.

"It is fine. Neisei and I think that it is better if the whole family were involved rather than hiding," Tudios replied. "Is the youngest one not coming?"

"Aya-*pi* is too young to understand any of this," Are said smiling.

"Yes, you're right," Tudios said. "Oh, before it gets cold, please try the tea."

Are looked excited and lifted the teacup.

"Its sweet mom," Jin said as he lifted his own cup to his lips, "and very good."

Are nodded and took a sip. Her husband followed.

"It takes me back to my birthplace… it's so nice," Are said sighing deeply. "You made a very nice choice Tudios-*pi*."

Tudios nodded.

"I thought you would like it Are-*pi*."

Jin watched as his mother and Xia's mother tittered away happily. His father and Xia's father looked at their wives almost amusedly. Jin turned his head to face Xia and she was holding her teacup sipping it politely. Her eyes rose to Jin's and she looked away quickly. Jin pouted. Why did she not speak the whole time? Jin thought for a moment. What did her father and mother call her?

"*Quelpi*…" Jin whispered, "…*quelpi.*"

There was silence in the room. Jin knew he said something wrong. He flushed, embarrassed.

"*Quelpi*," Neisei started, "means daughter."

Toi was smirking and Are was laughing without a care.

"Does it really?" Jin asked. He grinned and chuckled. Xia was his *quelpi*.

Neisei nodded and smirked.

"It does. But it does not matter. *Quelpi* when you train, teach him your language."

"Her language… sir?" Jin asked confused.

There was a short silence around the room.

"Ah down to business," Toi said. "May I, Neisei-*pi*?"
Neisei nodded.

"Although this is my house, he is your son." Neisei said. "Please explain what you can."

"You may have thought this already, Jin, but the Chang family is… not from Hainai. They are from Bluse."
Jin looked surprised but deep down he had a feeling that was the case. After all Xia could do something akin to magic.

"But isn't Bluse an Organization?" Jin asked.
Toi nodded.

"Yes, but it is a race first. All the organizations are first, well, civilizations."
Jin's eyes widened.

"And so that means the Chang family can also speak a different language," Toi explained.

"I see," Jin said unable to say anything else.

"Tohari-*kai*, you are going to be doing some things you have probably not even thought of," Tudios said softly. "But I believe you will do well. You are a kind boy after all."
Jin blushed.

"Thanks…" Jin said reddening.
Are laughed.

"And in due time, Jin, you will understand everything that is happening," Are said smiling. "Your father and I wait eagerly until that happens."
Jin nodded, still a little confused.

"Does that mean you two know different languages as well?" Jin asked his mother and father; who nodded.

"Naturally, when you work in a different area you learn its languages and customs. But that too, we'll have to explain another time," Toi said smiling. He flicked his long hair from his shoulder again and his wife gently stroked it.

"Tell us Jin," Are started, "are you ready to learn what Xia-*ken* has to offer?"

Jin was ready and fired up about the whole thing. He nodded and looked at Xia. She desperately wanted him *not* to be ready.

"I'm ready, so let's go!" Jin said smiling and looking at Xia. She scowled and turned away from Jin. That made Jin pout. He was in training to be *her* partner. He had to get her to like him somehow!

"Obviously it isn't working!" Jin said frustrated.

"Obviously you're not doing it right!" Xia snapped back.

Jin was thrown into practice the very same day he agreed he was ready to learn what Xia had to offer. He had no idea Black Rose had to practice so much in order to be good. Had he known what was about to be in store for him, he might have given himself a few more days to reconsider. Jin had only been with Xia for thirty minutes but was quickly finding out that she did not play around.

Xia was a slave driver, probably because she hated him so much, and she did not even take the time to understand where he was coming from.

"Do you just expect me to get it, *boom*, just like that?" Jin asked frustrated. He ran his fingers through his dampening black hair. "Geez, I bet even you didn't get it the first time around!"

Xia huffed.

"We cannot move on if you do not get this right Tohari! Now close your eyes and relax."

Jin grumbled and closed his eyes. He inhaled and exhaled, letting himself relax. After a minute of breathing nothing came into his mind and everything inside of him became peaceful.

"*Finally*," Xia breathed. "I can feel the tranquility in your body. Now dig deep and find something warm inside of you."

Jin sighed and dug into himself. He felt a tug at his body.

"Good. Now, do you see ribbons coming out of your body? Those are your magics."

Jin could see them, but were wound too tightly around his body for him to move. He could not struggle to loosen them. They were too tight, but they were not suffocating him.

"Can you see them? They should be floating around you," Xia's voice broke Jin's concentration.

Jin inhaled and exhaled and tried again. He dug deep within himself and found the ribbons. This time they were floating, just as Xia described.

"Yeah, I see them," Jin huffed. He did not realize he was so tired. "What now?"

"Push them out," Xia said. "Your magics should be outside of your body, ready to be used. Command your magics out of your body."

Jin opened his eyes and saw glowing white ribbons haloed around her. She looked beautiful.

"Good. See? Your magics are out and ready to be used."

Jin looked up and around him and noticed that black ribbons were glowing around him. He had no idea he had pushed them out. He grinned and reached to touch them. They were warm and soft, like velvet, but Jin could feel an indescribable strength in them. Was this the strength of his magic?

"Woah, are these things really my magic?" Jin asked surprised.

Xia nodded and caressed one of her snow-white ribbons.

"This is the raw form. The form that cannot only do the most damage, but can be damaged as well. When fighting, Tohari, we will not use the raw form. It could only harm you. We channel the magics into weaponry and fight like that. If weaponry does not work, then we fight with other forms of magics," Xia explained. "But for now, you are going to practice going in and out trying to gather your magics in a usable way."

Xia stood up.

"Where are you going?" Jin asked.

"To get us some tea. We are going to get dehydrated."

Jin nodded and closed his eyes. *She is really pretty.* Jin thought, as he felt his magics wrap around him and release something warm and pleasing inside of him.

"*Fadi...*" Xia said before she walked into the room. Neisei looked up at her and smiled.

"How is Tohari-*kai* doing?" Neisei asked.

"Fine," Xia replied. "He can meditate well enough and I told him that he needs to find a way to channel his magics into something useful in battle."

Neisei nodded.

"*Quelpi*, you know that takes time. Why are you being so hard on Tohari-*kai*? I find that he is a very nice boy."

Xia scoffed.

"He chased me for weeks and then rips off my mask! You expect me to be nice?" Xia asked angrily. "*Fadi* I do not want to treat this boy well."

Neisei sighed and turned to his daughter.

"Have you even thought that maybe he was put into your path to learn from you, and you from him?" Neisei asked.

Xia huffed and turned around.

"What do I have to learn from him?" she hissed and walked toward the kitchen.

Neisei smiled and turned back to his work.

"You still have so much to learn...*quelpi.*"

Toi walked out of the door to his left and smiled.

"Your collection always was better than mine," Toi said smiling.

Neisei looked up grinning.

"I'm sure it is," he said in his low voice.

Toi walked over to Neisei and placed a hand on his shoulder.

"I imagine they're going to be very close in the future."

"Yes. Maybe even *hanev*," Toi wagged his eyebrows in suggestion.

Neisei laughed.

"That would be a sight to behold... the two of them *bavdnah*."

"Who are *hanev*?" Are's voice came into the room followed by her body and Tudios'. Are looked at Toi and Neisei suspiciously.

"We are putting our faith in Jin. Hopefully he will melt Xia a little," Neisei said smiling.

"And the two of them *bavdnah*?" Tudios asked smiling.

Toi and Neisei nodded.

"It sounds like a lovely idea to me," Tudios said with amusement in her voice.

Xia nearly dropped the tray she was holding when she first stumbled onto Jin. He was in a sea of weapons and closing his eyes to materialize another one. Jin breathed in and a wave of ribbons flowed out of his hand forming a rod. Jin sighed and opened his eyes. A small shimmer of crimson flittered across his eyes. Xia blinked a couple of times. *I'm imagining things. I must be stressed*, Xia thought quickly.

"Look Xia! *Ha!* I made all these myself!" Jin said triumphantly.

Xia's eye twitched in annoyance.

"What gives you the right to call me by my first name?" she asked angrily.

Jin rolled his eyes.

"We're *partners*! I should think that we would be able to be on first name terms now," Jin said smiling. "Will Xia-*pi* do?"

"No!" Xia huffed angrily.

"Or would you rather I call you *bavdnah*?"

Xia's face flushed but a furious look was planted on it.

"You may *never* call me that!"

Jin was taken aback. Sure he did not know what the word meant, but surely it could not be that bad?

"Okay…" he muttered. "Xia-*pi* it is."

Xia was breathing hard and turned to calm herself.

"Your tea… is ready," he said in calm even tones.

Jin nodded and got up. He walked over to the tray and poured a cup of tea. The aroma was sweet and heady. Jin walked to the front of Xia and handed her a cup. She took it without looking at him.

"What no thanks?" he asked grinning.

"Do you expect a thank-you for every little thing?" she muttered angrily.

Jin grinned.

"That would be nice," he replied.

Xia scowled and stomped away from Jin.

"Well you are out of luck!" she said. "I am not going to be like one of your groupies."

Jin smiled.

"You know Xia-*pi*, I think I like working with you,"

Xia growled angrily.

"Well I don't like working with you! And clean up your mess!"

Jin laughed and started dematerializing weapons. There was silence until Jin finished.

"Xia-*pi*?" Jin asked.

Xia barely looked up while she sipped her tea but he knew she heard him.

"Tell me," Jin started, "what would happen if my ribbon broke?"

Xia continued sipping her tea.

"You would be in pain until it were fixed. You do not die unless they are all broken. And only a fool would die like that," Xia replied.

69

Jin nodded and poured himself a cup of tea. The sweetness and warmth made him feel that nostalgic feeling all over again.

"Xia-*pi*?"

"What?" Xia responded this time.

"What is it like in the outside world?" Jin asked.

"Is it relative to your training?"

"Maybe," Jin replied. "Make it under some random area of my study."

Xia sighed.

"The outside world… is more beautiful than this place. There are so many things to see and understand. I've only been to Bluse so it is all I know," she replied.

Jin nodded and smiled.

"I see… and do you miss your home?" Jin asked.

"Of course I do!" Xia snapped. "This is nothing compared to my home."

Jin shrugged and stretched.

"Well this is my only home. So I think it might compare very well."

Xia sipped her tea again.

"Fine," she said shortly.

Jin stared at Xia for a moment.

"What is Bluse?" Jin asked.

Xia nearly dropped her cup of tea.

"…Are you serious? Weren't you paying attention?"

Jin nodded. Xia rubbed her head.

"Bluse," Xia started, "is an Organization. It is where I come from."

"Organization of what? And how can you come from it?" Jin questioned. "Wait- what about it first being a civilization."

Xia sighing placed her teacup in its saucer and sat down. Jin followed.

"There are four Organizations in the outer world. Three of them are very well known and one is not. I come

70

from the Bluse Organization. It is something like the police in the outer world. Another Organization is the Raifelle, who are the unofficial leaders of the outer world. They use magics and other sorts of things like that. The Inikuria Organization is made up of spies. They find any information. Last is the Eracium Radical Organization…" Xia explained.

"I've heard of them!" Jin said excitedly. "The Andez are not well known and all the other Organizations fear them, right?"

"The Radicals are dangerous. It is right that we fear them," Xia said.

Jin looked thoughtful for a moment.

"The way I hear things… they are not to be feared. They are powerful but there is another side people must not know about," Jin said. "I don't know…"

"Okay, fine," she said. "But what is the point of you saying all of this? And asking all these questions?"

Jin sipped his tea, smiling warmly.

"You're my partner. This is important to you and I want to think this is the best way to get to know you… *bavdnah*."

Xia's eyes flashed dangerously.

"I am *not* your *bavdnah* nor will I ever be your *bavdnah*!" Xia cried furiously.

Jin smiled. He wondered what *bavdnah* meant anyway.

"Quelpi what is all the noise about?" Tudios asked walking into the room.

She smiled.

"Jin-*kai* you seem to be doing well. I can feel your magics all over the room. But be sure not to tire yourself out," Tudios said and Jin grinned. "Now *quelpi* tell me, what all the noise is about?"

Xia glared at Jin and turned to her mother.

"Tohari called me… *bavdnah*…" Xia muttered.

Tudios Chang looked at Xia and then Jin and then tittered.

"Oh my…" she laughed and turned to walk back out the door.

"*Moth!* Aren't going to say anything?" Xia whined. Tudios turned around grinning and giggling.

"Oh, well dear, why don't you explain to him what the word means?" Tudios suggested. Xia turned red and did not say a word.

"*Bavdnah!*" Tudios called. "*Bavdnah!*"

"My, my, what is all this?" Neisei asked walking into the room a few seconds later.

"It seems that Jin-*kai* has called *quelpi bavdnah*," Tudios explained still tittering away.

Neisei walked over to Jin and stared him in the eye. Jin found the man to be intimidating and his feeling of not wanting to upset the man came back. Was he not supposed to say that? Was he going to be told off?

Neisei Chang lifted a hand and Jin flinched. The next thing he felt was a strong hand clamped on his shoulder. Jin looked up, surprised. Neisei had a smile on his face and he gave Jin a pat on his shoulder. Jin was taken by surprise at the warm smile and gesture. Neisei smiled and walked back to his wife and took her arm.

"*Bavdnah* why don't we go downstairs, back to the other adults?" Neisei questioned lightly. "Or we could do something else… hm *bavdnah*?"

Neisei was putting more stress on *bavdnah,* but Jin still could not figure out what it meant.

"*Bavdnah*," Tudios said smiling, "we have *guests*. Perhaps after they leave?"

Neisei and Tudios laughed together and walked out of the room. Jin got the gist of what they were saying by the tones of their voices, but *bavdnah* was still a mystery to him. Xia was blushing and quickly exited to her room. Jin was left in the room with his question still unanswered.

Bavdnah

"*Bavdnah* means what?!" Jin choked on his drink.

"Lover, like I said," Are replied. "Are you alright?"

Jin nodded, still coughing. He called Xia his lover. A grin spread across his face. He laughed loudly.

"No *wonder* she was so upset with me," Jin said laughing. "Mom, I called Xia *bavdnah*. How funny is that?"

Are giggled.

"Very funny. Did you know that lover is different in Andez?"

"Andez?" Jin questioned.

Are nodded.

"Eracium Radical," she replied. "It really is called Andez by the people themselves. Eracium Radical was given to them because the Andez are different and radical to the laws of the other Organizations."

"That isn't fair…" Jin said. "Why were the Andez so disliked?"

Are twirled her long hair around her finger, looking thoughtful.

"It is believed that the Andez can cause terrible damage. The Organizations fear the power, so they stuck a name on the Andez and called them dangerous… not saying they aren't, Jin, but the Andez are just a different kind of people."

Jin looked thoughtful for a moment.

"Why do you know so much about the Andez?" Jin asked.

Are smiled.

"Your father and I base our studies around the Andez people. They are the ones with the most ruins, although, the ruins are also the hardest to find," Are explained. "But we also study other Organizations too."

"Oh… so then, how *do* you say lover in Andez?" Jin asked.

"*Hanev*," a manly voice replied.

Jin and Are looked towards the door.

"Toi-*pi*, you're up," Are said smiling and walking up to him.

"You're making too much noise," Toi said grinning. He kissed Are on the forehead tenderly. Jin smirked at his parents. They were so close to each other and they rarely fought. And when they did, it was kept within the room and they resolved it with a kiss or two. Jin wanted his marriage to be like theirs.

"I'm sorry, *hanev*," Are said softly. "Oh!"

Are lifted her husbands collar a little higher on his neck and Toi chuckled.

"Oh, it's alright," Toi said smiling. "I think he is old enough to understand *hanev*."

Jin looked interested.

"*Hanev*, dad? Do I want to know?" Jin asked.

Are smirked.

"Do you?"

Jin looked away blushing and quietly sipped his drink. Toi walked over to the table and sat down. Jin just noticed, as his father sat down, that he looked tired. His hair was a mess of waves and strands sticking out in odd angles down his back.

"Are you... alright?" Jin asked quietly.

Toi smiled.

"*Hanev*, could you bring me a cup of tea? The kind the Chang's gave us, if you don't mind."

Jin looked at his mom with wide eyes.

"You had the sweet tea and didn't tell me?" he accused. "You know how much I like it!"

Are smiled.

"Alright Jin, alright," Are said. "I'll give you some tea..."

Toi gave his wife a kiss and turned to Jin.

"Do you have another meeting with Xia-*ken*, today?" Toi asked.

Jin nodded.

"Yeah, but it's not until noon," he said. "In the meantime, I'm to go and meditate."

Toi nodded and smiled.

"As you should," Toi said tiredly. "You can't afford to be a burden to Xia-*ken*."

"I know," Jin said rolling his eyes. "I'm trying my best as it is."

Are placed a cup of tea in front of her husband and one in front of Jin. Then she sat down afterward. There was a comfortable silence. Jin happily sipped his tea and slipped into his nostalgic state. A tingle ran in his stomach and made him smile. Something inside of him tugged again, gripped him and made him want nothing more than to return to his home. Jin looked up and sighed.

"Is something wrong Jin?" Are asked, placing a hand on her son's shoulder.

Jin snapped out of his trance.

"Hu? No, I'm fine..." Jin muttered. He quickly drained his tea and stood up.

"You sure you're feeling alright?" Toi questioned. "Anything wrong, at all?"

Jin shook his head and grinned embarrassedly. He ran his fingers though his hair.

"Have you ever... had that feeling that you were missing your home? I mean, I feel like I'm missing it, but I'm right here," Jin said softly. Toi and Are smiled.

"Maybe you're just tired," Toi said warmly. "Don't overexert yourself."

Jin nodded.

"Of course," he smiled.

Toi and Are exchanged a glance.

"Jin," Are started, "in the future... there are going to be some things that you will have to face..."

Jin looked surprised.

"Woah, mom, you're getting a little serious over here," Jin said a little nervously.

"Listen Jin… whatever happens; do your best, okay?" Are said softly. Toi gently stroked Are's hair. She sighed softly.

"Mom, you don't have to worry about me. I can take care of myself."
Are nodded.

"I'm sure you can."

*   *   *

Jin finished his meditation and breathed deeply. Although he was at peace he felt a tugging at his body. It was not the same tugging he felt with his magics. This one felt deeper and not only pulled at his body, but his heart. The tugging sensation had been growing over weeks. Since he first started meditating and opening his magics. Still, no matter how good he was Xia would not even try to be cordial in the slightest. Jin was doing his very best and his teacher did not even show the slightest bit of encouragement. Maybe she was still upset about the *bavdnah* thing.

Jin got up from his sitting position and stretched. Desperate times called for desperate measures… and Jin was about ready to force Xia to be cordial. Jin readied himself before stepping outside of his house to go to Xia's.

The self-proclaimed detective passed his uncle on his way to Xia's house. Tekeda Tohari looked stressed but tried not to show it. There was a mass of armed forces behind him, waiting for instructions. Jin walked to his uncle and thanked him for everything he did for them.

"That's fine Jin," Tekeda said. "But if you don't mind, I'm a little busy right now."
Jin looked concerned.

"Why? What happened?" he asked.

76

Tekeda sighed deeply.

"Well… there's a leak in the wall. I wanted to know if your parents could figure anything out."

"Why would they need to figure anything out?" Jin questioned.

"The leak has a few inscriptions on it. Looks like outside world material to me. I don't want to have anything else to do with the outside world besides your parents… and neither does the rest of Hainai District. So we are contacting your parents now and seeing if they would assist us," Tekeda explained.

Jin looked at the police force behind Tekeda in question. There were many more there than seemed necessary.

"Why are there so many men here?" Jin inquired to his uncle.

"We are all going down to the leak and seeing what has opened up because of it. I fear that *things* from the outside world might come into our perfect space."

Jin chuckled. *If it were so perfect, police would not be needed… nor would Black Rose,* Jin thought.

"Oh… do you think the inscriptions could be causing the leak?" Jin asked after a few more seconds of thought. "Or maybe keeping it open? Something from the outside world might be trying to get in… but why?"

"I don't know. That's why I'm asking your parents!" Tekeda snapped. "Now that you've played detective, why don't you run off to where you were going."

"…Alright," Jin muttered and turned to go on his way.

"Try not to get involved in this one…" Tekeda called to Jin.

"Can't make any promises!" Jin called back. He walked to Xia's house excitedly. Maybe he would be able to solve this with Black Rose! He was better than ever in controlling his magics now! He could even fight with the weapons he created, after a few weeks of intense training and better than that, he could defend himself against almost anything. Even Neisei

77

and Tudios said that he learned faster than anyone else they knew and that his application of skill was better than Xia's (although he was not to rub it in her face). Still Xia had no intention of showing Jin that she thought he was doing a good job.

Maybe a little persuasion from her bavdnah *might change her mind,* Jin thought grinning. *Or maybe not... She might kill me if I tried to make a move on her. But still, if I don't who will? And it's not like she isn't a girl in there somewhere! She has to have thought of a guy sometime in her life... Maybe not a* bavdnah *but something inside of her must want* some *kind of affection!*

Jin's mind was racing furiously with ways to get Xia to befriend him as he walked to the Chang household. Jin knocked on the door and Tudios answered it, smiling kindly. She was dressed smartly, as usual and Jin started to wonder if she and his mother had conversed lately. They were very much alike- but so different at the same time. Tudios was calm and reflective while Are was excited about every little thing.

"Ah, Jin-*kai* how are you today?" Tudios asked kissing both of Jin's cheeks. He was finally used to it after the many weeks of his training in the Chang house.

"I'm good. How're you?" Jin asked.
Tudios smiled.

"Same as always. Neisei-*pi* is in the study. *Quelpi* is out shopping for us. She will return in a few minutes. I will bring you your favorite tea when it is ready."
Jin nodded.

"That would be great, thanks," Jin smiled. He made his way to the study and knocked on the door. Neisei opened it seconds later. His head was wrapped in bandages. The scar was covered up. Jin wanted to ask what happened but thought better of it.

"Jin-*kai* it is a pleasure to see you. *Quelpi* is out but I will be glad to entertain you in her stead. Come in."

Jin could only nod. Every time he was with Neisei he found himself in awe and a little intimidated. Jin followed Neisei to the study and sat down on one of the chairs.

"It's a scar from a long time ago," Neisei replied to Jin's unspoken question. "I lost a fight and paid the price."

"I-I see," Jin managed. He did not even realize he had been staring.

"It's been bleeding lately. I thought to seal it up before it got infected," Neisei said with a smile, disregarding Jin's embarrassment. "So how do you enjoy your training so far?"

"I like it very much, but Xia's not very encouraging," Jin replied honestly.

Neisei nodded.

"Yes, she is a little too harsh with her mouth and not kind enough with her actions, but I am hoping you will help her with that," he said softly.

"Me sir?" Jin questioned.

"Please, call me Neisei. And yes, you," Neisei replied. "You have a personality that makes *quelpi* what to clam up. But at the same time it challenges her to be better."

Jin looked surprised.

"I do?" he asked. "I really just think she… doesn't like me very much."

Neisei chuckled.

"I believe, that in time, you two will be very good friends," he said softly. "It has been a very long time since *quelpi* has had any good friends."

Jin felt that tug again.

"Really?" he asked. "Then I'll have to do my best to make her my friend!"

A soft feminine giggle floated into the room.

"Please do, Jin-*kai*. That would be most excellent," Tudios said placing a cup of tea in front of her husband, then one in front of Jin. Jin smiled inhaling the scent of the tea and letting the aroma take him far away.

"You really are being impossible!" Xia huffed.

Jin cocked an eyebrow. They were supposed to be meditating but the two of them were bickering instead. Xia had her magics extended so they haloed around her. Jin's black ribbons were open wide as well.

"Why?" he asked. "Because you don't like what I have to say? Or is it something else, hm?"

Xia looked at Jin sourly. Jin grinned.

"Why… are you looking at me like that?" Xia asked carefully.

Jin's grin became wider.

"Like what?" he questioned.

"Like that! Stop looking at me like that!" Xia snapped. Jin leaned closer. His ribbons glided forward. Xia scooted back.

"I asked you what look I was giving you," Jin said, "and you didn't respond."

His voice sounded deeper almost, seductive. Xia glared at him in annoyance.

"If you don't stop leaning toward me…" she threatened. Jin grinned and leaned in closer, but this time his magics darted forward and wrapped around Xia's body and her white ribbon. Xia yelped in surprise as her body became wound tight and her back was pressed against the floor. Her own magics dashed toward Jin and bound him tightly as well. He let out his own cry as they pulled him forward and suspended his face less than an inch above Xia. The rest of his body was crouched over hers, tied tightly by her magics. His body felt electrified as her ribbons tightened around his body. If either of them moved…

"Jin Tohari! Undo this mess immediately!" Xia growled unable to move.

Jin laughed.

"I have no idea what just happened! But I must admit, this is pretty comfortable," he said grinning. Xia looked furious.

"Tohari!" she yelled "If you don't-"

"Shh!" Jin said quickly. "Don't be too loud! What if your parents hear you and see what is going on? What will they think if they see us in this position? Use your head for a moment!"

Xia looked like she considered it and lowered her voice.

"You better not move or else I'll kill you!"

"You're one to be making threats seeing as you're tied under *me*," Jin said grinning.

"Thank goodness you brushed your teeth before you came... I wouldn't know what to do if you didn't," Xia muttered.

"You'd probably have to suck it up. But if you hadn't noticed, I can smell your breath too," Jin countered. "By the way your breath smells like my favorite tea. Mind if I have a taste?"

Xia's face flushed.

"Yes I mind if you have a taste!" she shrieked.

"Shh, okay, okay!" Jin said quickly. "I was joking geez..."

Xia fumed, but she was still red.

"Is anything wrong up there?" Tudios' voice suddenly called.

Xia's eyes became wide.

"No! No, we're fine!" she said quickly.

"...Okay," Tudios' voice said after a few seconds.

Jin sighed.

"That was-"

"Too close..." Xia sighed. She looked surprised for a second.

Jin noticed.

"What's wrong?" he asked concerned.

"Did you feel that?" she asked.

"What?" Jin replied.

"They're loosening!"

Jin didn't feel anything different.

"No they aren't, mine are still-"

The ribbons around Jin suddenly disappeared and he fell right into Xia's open lips. There was a shocked silence and nothing moved. Then suddenly Jin felt a stinging on his cheek.

Xia slapped him.

Jin held his cheek with wide eyes.

"What was that for?!" he cried.

"You kissed me!" she answered shocked as much as he was.

"I did not! I just fell!"

"You *kissed* me! Your lips fell right into mine!"

"It was *your* magics that released me, so blame it on yourself! *You* kissed *me!*"

"I would never do such a thing!"

"I knew you wanted to be my *bavdnah!*"

"Don't flatter yourself Jin Tohari! I would not be caught dead!"

Xia and Jin glared murder at each other. Jin held his stinging cheek and Xia's hand was to her mouth.

"My, my, what is all this?" Neisei asked walking into the room. He was met with silence and sighed.

"I guess then nothing is wrong," Xia's father said in his deep voice. Jin and Xia did not say anything and continued to stare at each other in anger.

"I am sorry for disturbing the lesson," Neisei said walking out of the room.

Jin and Xia stared at each other for the remainder of the lesson.

∗   ∗   ∗

Toi and Are returned to their home in the evening. Jin was waiting for his parents so he could tell them how his day went. He rubbed his cheek in recollection. Xia hit hard, but she tasted like sweet tea... It was all worth it in Jin's opinion.

Her face was flushed and she lost control around him again. Maybe Neisei was right. He was good at bringing out the different sides in Xia.

A delicious aroma spread throughout the house as Jin prepared dinner. His mom and dad would be pleased and would not be allowed to keep all the information about the leak a secret. Jin desperately wanted to know what was going on, since his uncle would say nothing to him. Jin took the pan off the burner and took out a bowl. He gently shook the pan and the contents slid out. A few seconds later, he heard the door open and heard his mother's voice.

"Oh wow, it smells great in here!" she said. She laughed and said her husband's name.

"I think a young man is trying to kiss up to us. I wonder what the reason is," Jin's father's voice said with mirth. "Shall we go entertain him?"

Jin heard his mother's laugh again. He rolled his eyes and placed the bowl on the table. He was not exactly sure he wanted to know what they were saying other than what was loud enough for him to hear.

"Jin! It looks great!" Are said as she looked at the food on the table.

Jin grinned.

"It tastes good too," he said. "Let's eat."

His parent's laughed and sat around the table.

"Is Aya sleeping?" Toi asked.

Jin nodded.

"I made her something else and she went right to sleep after it," Jin said smiling. "She was exhausted and nearly fell asleep at the table."

Are and Toi laughed.

"Poor thing, but nothing some sleep can't cure," Toi said. "We'll check on her later."

Toi took a bite out of his food.

"This is very good Jin. Very well seasoned," he remarked.

Jin grinned.

"Thanks," he said. "So what'd you find out about the leak?"

Are laughed.

"Right to the point I see," she grinned. "Well, since you can't possibly wait any longer, the leak really isn't a leak at all. It's an illusion made by the inscription on the wall."

"How do inscriptions make illusions?" Jin asked.

"Simple," Toi said. "The inscriptions are made from a magic source. The magic source was sent out to accomplish a goal. In this case, the goal was to send a message to certain people."

"Who?" Jin asked intrigued.

Are took a sip of her drink and Toi continued eating. They did not reply.

"Who? Who?" Jin asked again. Jin groaned in frustration. His mom finally cracked a smirk.

"Do you remember the prophecy we told you about a few weeks past?" Are asked.

Jin nodded.

"What about it?" he inquired back.

"The inscription was sent to the lovers, but it seems that Toi and I sufficed to read the message."

"Wait, so the lovers that the ruins were talking about are in Hainai? Shouldn't we be looking for them or something?" Jin asked excited. "Couldn't they be trouble for the people in Hainai District?"

Toi nodded.

"Yes, but Are and I think that the inscription was made to warn the lovers, not to bring destruction to Hainai District," Toi explained. "Right after Are and I figured out what the inscription said, it disappeared."

Jin still looked concerned.

"What did the inscription say?" Jin asked after a few minutes of silence.

"The lovers are going to face some troubles in the future, but in order to bring honor and peace home they need to persevere," Toi replied softly. "It was something like that. Jin, nothing has come from this yet, so do not jump into it until it needs to be jumped into."

Jin cocked his head to the side a little. His parents didn't usually tell him not to do something, it made him curious, but he was not going to go disobey his parents. He had too much on his plate to deal with, without his parents being mad at him.

"So Jin, aside from our obviously boring day, how was yours?" Are asked.

Jin grinned and blushed a little.

"Well… it was… um… interesting…" Jin mumbled.

Toi cocked an eyebrow.

"Was it now? Why do you say that?" he asked.

Jin laughed nervously and ran his fingers through his hair.

"I accidentally kissed… Xia…."

Silence filled the room. Jin's face flushed when Are laughed loudly.

"Are you serious, Jin?" she asked smiling. "*Accidentally*? How did that happen?"

"It *really* wasn't my fault!" Jin said quickly. "We were meditating and then my magics sort of attacked hers and we ended up all bound and I was on top of her. We were stuck like that and then out of nowhere, the magics decided they wanted to give out and I fell on her and we sort of… kissed."

Jin explained what happened all very quickly. Are and Toi listened the best they could and laughed.

"I'm not going to even try to understand what you said," Toi said rubbing his head.

"I am! So let me get this straight. You were meditating, right? And then something happened with your magics, they bonded together, let's say. And then you were bound with Xia for a time and when it finally released, you fell onto her and kissed her, am I right?" Are concluded.

Jin nodded embarrassed. Are laughed again.

"That is the funniest thing I've heard all day! Toi-*pi*, isn't this great?" Are asked with twinkling eyes. Toi nodded smiling.

"Very funny indeed. I daresay the two of them will be best friends soon," Toi said smiling. His long fingers stretched and stroked the back of his wife's hand tenderly. Are closed her eyes. Jin looked at his mother and saw how peaceful she looked. He wondered how his father managed to quell his overly excited wife with a simple touch. Jin watched his parents without saying a word. Something about the way his father moved closer to his mother while not losing the stroking rhythm of his fingers and the way his mother rested her head against his father's shoulder, knowing he would be there, mesmerized him. Could two people really be this peaceful? Jin could almost *feel* the serenity waft about the room. It even soothed him.

Jin had to know.

"Dad…" Toi opened his eyes and looked at Jin. "How are you doing that?'

"Doing what?" Toi asked softly.

"You're like… making the whole room feel relaxed," Jin replied. His father smiled.

"I'm really only calming your mother, but because you are watching the movement, it is making you relaxed," Toi explained quietly. "Here give me your hand, but I can't guarantee you'll feel the same."

"Why not?" Jin asked handing over his hand. His father took it and gently started to stroke the back of it.

"It is the language of touch," Toi replied.

Jin felt his eyes fall to a close. The rhythm was slow and gentle. Jin let himself relax completely.

"What do you mean I won't feel the same?" he asked. "I'm close to sleeping already!"

Toi chuckled.

"If I did to you what I am doing to your mother, well, let's just say you would feel a bit uncomfortable," Toi said softly.

"How can you do two things at once?" Jin asked sleepily.

"Practice," Toi replied.

Are giggled softly.

"Jin when you are in Toi-*pi*'s place you'll understand. But for right now, just let it relax you…"

"What if I'm never in dad's place?" Jin asked drifting in between sleep and awake.

Toi chuckled, "Someday you… both of you will be in my place."

Jin closed his eyes and drifted off to sleep.

First Sign

Jin watched Xia put on her mask and change into Black Rose. Her hair became pitch black and wavy. Jin turned around when her clothes started to shine. He knew they were changing into her Black Rose attire.

Xia gave Jin the message that something was going on at the mayor's mansion at seven. He had just finished all the transportation practices Xia gave him minutes before the two of them came in contact with one another. Jin had rushed over to Xia's house only to find out that he was about to go on his first mission.

Jin heard Xia scowl and he turned around.

"Don't flatter yourself." Black Rose said as she walked past Jin. "I'm not getting naked or anything... although you would like that wouldn't you, kiss stealer?"

Jin rolled his eyes while he crossed his arms in front of his chest.

"Are you still upset over that? I would have thought we could be mature about this," Jin said.

"Mature? You *stole* my first kiss!"

Jin smirked.

"I didn't know you cared about that kind of stuff, Black Rose!"

Black Rose did not reply but Jin could tell he was grating her nerves.

"I do not usually. But since it was *you* I was forced to reconsider," she said.

"Well then I am glad to have stolen your first kiss," Jin said chuckling.

Black Rose muttered something that Jin did not catch. Before he could even joke on her Black Rose's face turned serious. The time for joking was over.

"Alright Tohari listen up. The police cannot do anything about the hostage because of the possibility that the hostage might become injured. The criminals are expecting me, but not you. So you will attack when I call for it. *No sooner.* We cannot afford mistakes and at all costs you-"

"Cannot use magics. I know, I know!" Jin said exasperatedly. "We can't let on that we are from the outer world, yada, yada."

Black Rose nodded.

"Fine. Let's go."

Black Rose led Jin on top of rooftops and through alleyways until they reached their destination. The police force was everywhere waiting for a chance to go in. Jin saw his uncle and smirked. He was going to have a cow when he found out what Jin was doing. Black Rose looked at the police and then at the building.

"Tohari, come here," she whispered. Jin walked over to her.

"Yeah?"

"We are transporting there. Hold onto me," Black Rose said quickly. Before Jin had a response Black Rose grabbed his arm and transported them both out of the alley where they were hiding. Jin's feet landed on something hard and when he looked down, it was the roof. Black Rose had her hand covering his mouth. Jin nodded telling her he would be quiet and she released him. He looked around and saw that they faced the garden. The Police were facing the other side and could not see them.

"Tohari, the hostage is right below us, listen."

Jin went onto his knees and heard voices.

"What do we do?" he asked.

"We have to wait until the best moment," Black Rose replied. "I will go in and confront the criminals. You keep watch and stop whoever tries to get away. There are only four people."

Jin nodded. Screams were heard from below. That was Black Rose's cue.

"This is your first mission. Don't screw up," Black Rose said walking to the edge of the room. A large window was below her. Jin smirked.

"Don't get caught," he said. Black Rose nodded and jumped through the open window. Jin sat still and listened to her say a few lines. Jin heard more yelling. Two voices- no three. Jin strained to listen then heard cries of pain. *Black Rose seems to be dishing out a butt whipping,* Jin thought grinning. Suddenly, a mass of black flew out of the window and rolled onto the ground.

"You're not getting away!" Black Rose cried. Jin knew that was his cue. He took a running start and jumped. The adrenaline flowed through his veins as he rolled on the ground and stopped the man dead in his tracks.

"Going somewhere?" Jin asked as he stood ready to attack.

The man was dressed in black from head to toe and wore a full facemask. He growled.

"Stupid punk! Get out of the way!" he yelled and whipped out his gun. Jin's heart skipped a beat. He knew how to handle people with guns. He was a self-proclaimed detective after all. He *had* to know how to defend himself!

"You're not getting away!" Jin cried. The man jerked and aimed his gun. Jin, without a second's hesitation, rushed forward and aimed for the man's legs. The criminal stumbled and Jin jumped to knock the gun out of his hand. It flew out of his hand and onto the grass.

"Why you little-"

Jin quickly turned and kicked the man in the face. Something snapped and the criminal fell to the floor, unconscious. Jin grinned. He looked towards the open window and saw Black Rose punching another person, dressed in black in the face. She jumped into the garden and Jin dove into a thicket of nicely arranged bushes. He was not supposed to be seen. Jin watched as Black Rose handled another criminal with ease. He fell to the ground. Jin did a silent cheer and started counting the criminals that were unconscious. Two in the garden and one in the mansion. That made three… Jin's mouth opened in horror.

"Black Rose, watch out!"

BANG!

Jin's eyes widened. That was a gunshot. His hands started shaking. Black Rose fell to the ground. A man came out from the side of the building with his gun raised. Jin could feel the smirk on his face.

"Black Rose… the new heroine from the shadows," the man said. "It seems you've finally been caught."

Black Rose grit her teeth.

"Don't bet your luck," she growled. "I'll get out of this on my own."

The man laughed,

"You've already lost it!" he shot another bullet, Black Rose cringed, but it just nicked her leg. "I think I'm going to just get it over with."

"Yeah, right after you finish torturing me, you low-life," Black Rose scowled. The man grinned and pointed his gun at Black Rose's head.

Jin's heart was pounding. He had to save Black Rose! He shot up with his hands trembling. *He had to save Black Rose!* Jin ran out of the bushing charging towards the man.

"Try killing her when I'm *not* watching!" Jin roared and struck the man with his fist. The man let out a startled cry and fell.

"Let's see how you like this!" Jin cried and knocked the man flat on his back. He kicked the gun out of his hand. Panic was overriding Jin's system. Black Rose is going to get hurt. He *shot* Black Rose!

"You shot… Black Rose…" Jin growled angrily. The man whimpered hopelessly on the ground. Jin did not know exactly what he was doing. All he knew is that the man injured Black Rose and he was going to pay.

"Shut-up!" Jin cried and delivered a swift kick to the man's head, unable to take the helpless noises any longer. Jin left the man unconscious.

"*Tohari!*" Black Rose cried shocked. Jin turned slowly to Black Rose. His eyes flickered crimson. She gasped. This was the second time that happened. It could not be a trick her eyes were playing on her anymore. She had to regain her control over him.

"Tohari what are you doing?" Black Rose asked angrily. "You were about to over do it!"

"I didn't did I?" Jin asked. Black Rose could tell there was something darker in his voice. Something trembled inside of her.

"I could have handled it. Didn't you hear me?" Black Rose said angrily. She slowly tried to get up but fell back down with a cry.

"You can't even lift yourself up," Jin muttered. He walked over to Black Rose and knelt to her. She flinched away from him. Jin's eyes softened but the crimson shimmer was still there.

"Are you afraid of me?" he questioned softly. Black Rose was not sure if he was talking about himself or someone else.

"Of course not!" she huffed. Jin grinned.

"Alright then, hold on."

Jin placed an arm under Black Rose's leg and another around her waist. Black Rose grudgingly held onto him.

"What are you planning to do?" Black Rose asked wearily.

"Transport."

Black Rose visibly panicked.

"Then let me go! I do not want to end up on the other side of Hainai!"

Jin looked down at Black Rose with a grin on his face. Black Rose's eyes widened when Jin started to disappear with her in his arms. She was going to kill him if she got out alive. This *was* his first transportation.

*   *   *

Jin landed on grassy ground and saw that it was the park. He gently placed Black Rose on a stone bench, trying not to injure her further.

"See there was nothing for you to worry about," Jin said grinning. "I knew what I was doing."

Black Rose stared at Jin in disbelief. Jin chucked and reached for his partner's feet. His fingers moved to her boot and started to untie them.

"What are you doing?" Black Rose asked. She was blushing but in the dim light of the park it was hardly visible. Jin grinned.

"I'm only removing your boot, *bavdnah,*" Jin said grinning. Black Rose rolled her eyes.

"Don't flatter yourself," she muttered softly. Jin removed the boot and placed it on the ground.

"I'll make sure I do," he smiled. Jin examined Black Rose's leg carefully. He gently pressed on the areas around the cuts and Black Rose winced.

"Be careful!" she whispered furiously. Jin paid her no attention.

"You're lucky both bullets only cut the surface," Jin said matter-of-factly. "I'll just wrap it so it doesn't get infected."

"The house is right down the street," Black Rose muttered. "I can walk."
Jin took out a handkerchief out of his pocket.

"Can you?" he questioned. "It may not be very deep but bullets aren't friendly when they hit you and getting grazed hurts more than the bullet actually in you."

"Matter of opinion…" Black Rose muttered. Jin ignored her.

Black Rose scoffed and looked out towards the small pond. She was embarrassed. Jin searched in his pockets and found a small hand cleaner. Black Rose turned her head back to Jin after hearing him digging in his pockets.

"What, do you have everything in there?" Black Rose asked.

Jin shrugged.

"Best be prepared," he said. Jin dabbed some cleaner on Black Rose's wounds and she flinched.

"Don't be a baby," Jin grinned. He wrapped the handkerchief around Black Rose's wound and tied it tight.

"A little gentler, please?" she muttered angrily.

Jin laughed.

"There, all done. You were a good patient. Would you like a piece of candy?" Jin asked pinching Black Rose on her cheeks.

"Do not mock me," she pouted.

Jin laughed and took her boot off the ground. She helped him get it back on.

"I've always wondered how you fought in heels," Jin said grinning.

Black Rose rolled her eyes and moved to stand up. Her injured leg wobbled and she jerked forward. Jin caught her and stood her upright.

"Be careful Black Rose," he whispered. "Just because you think you're invincible, it doesn't mean you are."

Black Rose huffed and tried moving again. She wobbled and held onto Jin.

"Geez. You're so stubborn," Jin muttered. In one swift movement he lifted Black Rose onto his back.

"Let me down!" Black Rose cried blushing.

Jin shrugged and adjusted Black Rose on his back.

"If you weren't so stubborn, then it would not be embarrassing," Jin said. "Now let's go drop you off."

"Not like this!" Black Rose whimpered.

"*Yes* like this. You can't walk and as much as you want me to leave you here, it's not going to happen," Jin said walking slowly down the quiet street. Black Rose huffed, but did not say anything for a while and Jin concentrated on walking slow enough not to aggravate Black Rose's leg.

"Tohari…" Black Rose's voice was quiet even when breaking the silence.

"Yeah?" Jin asked.

Black Rose did not say anything for a long time. Jin thought she might have fallen asleep.

"…You did well today," Black Rose said finally, "good enough to be my partner…"

Jin grinned widely.

"Really? Do you mean it?" he asked excitedly. "Say it again."

"Don't bother asking me to say it again. I will not," Black Rose said simply.

Jin laughed overjoyed. He was now officially Black Rose's partner! Black Rose muttered something unintelligible.

"You can't take it back now!" Jin said.

Black Rose groaned.

"*Please* shut your mouth. I am starting to regret saying anything at all," she muttered.

"Shut-up you complainer," Jin said grinning. "I'm going to work harder now so you don't have to worry."

"What exactly do you think I am worried about?" Black Rose wanted to wring Jin's neck. "For all I know, you will make a mess of Hainai District, reveal my identity and force me to live in some other bubble in the outside world."

Jin laughed and adjusted Black Rose on his back again.

"Then I will chase you again, unmask you again and make you partner up with me, rather than choosing death."

Jin could tell Black Rose was scowling.

"Idiot…" she muttered.

"*Bavdnah!*" Jin countered.

Black Rose growled.

"I am *not* your *bavdnah*!"

Second Sign

The school bell rang and Jin sighed as his class started packing up their books. His days here seemed almost… boring. He and Xia still fought, but it was only to keep up appearances. She still disliked him, to be sure, but it was not the intense hate like before. Fighting alongside Black Rose was second nature to him now, after weeks of crime busting.

Jin looked out the window watching the cold settle in. It would be snowing soon. Jin closed his eyes and imagined walking in the snow, letting it fall into his hair, trying to eat it. Jin chuckled and looked to his side. The class cleared out all except Xia. Jin smiled at her.

"No after school allowed today. Are we going to your house or mine?" Jin asked.

Xia shrugged.

"I do not have a preference. I'm going to beat you either way," Xia said pushing in her chair. Jin stood up.

"I feel lucky today," he said. "I might actually win."

Xia rolled her eyes.

"How many times must I ask you *not* to push your luck?" Xia asked walking towards the door. Jin followed and tucked his arms behind his head. His bag dangled loosely in his fingers.

"At least a million times," he replied grinning. "But you'll just have to go for a million more. I'll meet you at the gate."

Xia nodded, opening her locker. A letter fell out of it. Xia stared at it while it was on the floor. Jin, still standing next to Xia, rolled his eyes and walked over to her and picked it up. It was feather light. Xia stared at it while Jin examined it. She did not look keen on opening it.

"This reminds me of something I received a few days ago," Jin said thoughtfully.

Xia looked serious.

"Did you open it?" she asked. Jin shook his head a little worried by her tone of voice.

"No... but I think I still have it," he said searching in his bag. He found the letter and waved it in front of Xia's face grinning. She snatched it without a word and ripped it open.

"Hey! What're you doing?" Jin cried surprised. "You can't just go opening other people's letters!"

Xia ignored him and took out the piece of paper that was inside. One word was written on it.

Ikelidek

Jin stared at the word with wide eyes. A pain seared through him, tearing at his heart. He clutched his chest and doubled over. Jin felt as if knives were stabbing at him, cutting him. His heart was pounding madly and he felt the tugging become tighter than ever.

"Tohari!" Xia cried surprised. She knelt down and held Jin's shoulders. He was shaking.

"Tohari are you alright?" Xia asked panicked and confused. His breath was ragged and it sounded as if he just ran for miles. Jin lifted his head slowly. Xia covered her mouth with her hand in shock. He was sweating like he had a fever and he was paler than usual, but that was not what shocked Xia. His eyes were red. Crimson like blood and they pierced her as soon as they reached her. This was the third time she saw his eyes like this. Jin gripped Xia's shoulders so tight she winced but she still held onto him. She was frightened for him. Slowly he reached out a hand towards the letter in Xia's.

"Destroy it..." he whispered harshly. "Get *rid* of it!"

Xia looked down at Jin with fright. Something was wrong with him and she needed him to get over it. He was frightening her.

"Get a *hold* of yourself!" she said sharply. "What is wrong with you?"

"*Give me the letter!*" Jin reached for the paper and as soon as it reached his fingers it burned to ashes.

Xia's eyes went wide.

"Tohari you idiot! You just destroyed something important!"

Jin looked up at Xia again. She fell wide-eyed and silent. Those eyes… were not of Hainai. A pained expression fell across Jin's features and he closed his eyes. His head fell onto Xia's shoulder helplessly.

"What…are you doing?" Xia whispered shocked.

Jin's grip on Xia's arms loosened slightly. His breathing was shallow and shaky.

"Don't move…" his voice softly pleaded. His voice sounded like Jin again, but it was different. Xia felt moisture seep through her uniform.

Having Jin resting on her shoulder was a different kind of contact than what she was used to but she did not want to upset him further. Whatever that word meant, it aggravated Jin. Xia had to admit, it was kind of scary to see him like that- whatever *that* was.

"Are you alright?" Xia questioned after a minute. Jin's breathing was back to normal and she did not want him to think she was being overly indulgent.

Jin nodded into her shoulder. It was frightening to see Jin light that. Xia was glad she was able to calm him but why was he so upset in the first place?

"If you are fine, then get off me," Xia huffed. "What if someone sees? I don't need people having ideas about us."

Jin chuckled and sat up. He ran his fingers through his damp hair and gazed at the door.

"Thanks," he muttered. He opened his eyes and all traces of crimson were gone leaving behind his honey colored orbs.

Xia sighed standing up.

"Do not… worry about it," she said softly. "Perhaps you should go home and rest?"

"…Maybe."

For once in her life Xia Chang was worried for Jin Tohari.

"Can you walk?" she asked.

Jin shrugged and did not bother standing up. A helpless expression was on his face. Xia gazed down at him with worry. Jin's behavior confused and unnerved her. Xia thought of something to make Jin smile.

"Do you need a piggyback?" Xia asked not liking the way Jin was looking. A small smirk played on Jin's lips. A small sense of triumph flittered through Xia.

"Are you trying to cheer me up?" Jin asked grinning like normal. "I'm flattered, *bavdnah*."

Xia's eye twitched and she was sorry she even tried to cheer Jing up. She scowled.

"Don't flatter yourself!" Xia huffed and walked towards the exit.

Jin grinned and stood up. He took his bag off the floor and jogged to catch up to Xia, dusting himself off the whole time.

"So were you *really* worried about me, *bavdnah*?" Jin asked grinning. "Honestly I'm flattered."
Xia glared at Jin.

"It will never happen again," she snapped. "So do not expect special treatment from me!"
Jin grinned. *Whatever you say*, he thought.

*　　*　　*

Jin closed his eyes and flopped on his bed. He felt exhausted. Minutes passed and Jin did not open his eyes. A sore area had welled in his chest and bothered him. Jin rolled over onto his back. He rubbed at the soreness trying to will it to disappear. It felt as if it was inside of him rather than on him and his rubbing did not do anything to soothe it. Jin let out an aggravated yell and sat up. There was a gentle knock on his door. Jin looked towards the noise and saw his mother smiling at him. She was holding a cup of tea.

"You want some? I just made it," Are said smiling. Jin nodded. His mother walked into the room and set the cup of tea on the table. She sat on her son's bed and held his hand.

"Is something the matter?" she asked after a minute.

Jin sighed looking at the steam from the tea rise and disappear into the air. He wished the pain would disappear as the steam did.

"...Today in school... I think I nearly collapsed... I think." Jin explained quietly. "I don't know what happened exactly. All I remember is feeling a lot of pain then feeling it fade away when I held onto Xia..."

Are listened quietly and waited for Jin to continue.

"I don't know if I said anything... or if I did something... I can't remember anything really well at all," Jin covered his face with his free hand, "...and I feel this throbbing pain in my chest. It's just sitting there...hurting."

"Did you do something at school to injure yourself?" Are Tohari asked concerned.

Jin shook his head.

"No. We didn't have gym so I didn't get beat up by Xia today," Jin chuckled darkly. "It was after school... I was at Xia's locker. A letter fell out of it..."

Jin gasped.

"Geez I remember now!" Jin turned to him mom. "I letter fell out of Xia's locker and I told her that I had received one a few days earlier. She asked me if I still had it and I showed it to her... she opened it... and I...I felt this pain tear through me... I don't remember after that until I was holding onto Xia."

Are ran her hand though her son's hair tenderly.

"Do you remember what it said?" she asked. "Anything at all."

Jin closed his eyes in pain and nodded.

"It was only one word."

"Did you know what it meant?"

Jin shrugged.

"I *know* I've never seen the word before, but at the same time I knew it and it tore me apart."

Are nodded and hugged her son to her.

"What was the word?" she questioned. Jin didn't know if he wanted to say it for fear of blanking out again.

"...*Ikelidek.*"

There was silence in the room. Jin looked up to find his mother crying.

*   *   *

"*Quelpi,* what is wrong? You look distressed," Neisei Chang asked his daughter. Xia lifted one hand to her cheek while the other hand slipped an envelope into her desk drawer.

"Really? I hadn't noticed," Xia muttered softly.

Neisei walked over to Xia worried.

"Did something happen?" he asked.

Xia nodded.

"Yes, but I do not understand why."

Neisei sat next to his daughter lifting her chin to have her face him.

"What do you mean?"

Xia sighed and held her father's hand.

"Why was he crying?" she asked her father quietly. "Why was his reaction so severe?"

Neisei smiled gently at Xia.

"Are you referring to Jin-*kai?*" Neisei asked.

Xia nodded.

"I cannot understand him... or what has happened to him."

"What happened?"

Xia sighed and let go of her father's hand.

"I opened a letter addressed to Tohari today. He acted strangely... he started crying. He looked as if he was in so much pain."

Neisei's smile faded.

"Was it because of the contents of the letter?" he asked. "Did Tohari-*kai* not like what it said?"

Xia almost chuckled.

"He hated what it said. He burned the letter to nothing…. I do not know what to do."

"Are you afraid that Tohari is injured? Did you check to see if he was alright?"

Xia nodded.

"I could not do anything for him. He read the letter and just… he just lost *himself*. When he held onto me he finally seemed to come to his senses. *Fadi* I could not do anything for him."

Neisei gently stroked his daughter's back.

"What you did was enough. Tohari-*kai* came to his right mind you said after held you. This means that whatever made him upset you took that away," Neisei said softly. "May I ask what was in the letter that made Tohari-*kai* so upset?"

Xia looked uncertain.

"I do not wish for it to unsettle you, although, you might know what it means."

Neisei nodded.

"Thank-you for taking my welfare into consideration, but I believe I will do better if you told me the root of your unhappiness."

Xia nodded.

"The letter only had one word. *Ikelidek*," Xia said. "Do you know what that means?"

Neisei stood up nodding faintly.

"*Quelpi* I am thanking you for telling me what the letter said, but never say that word to Tohari-*kai*."

"I understand *fadi*, but what does it mean?" Xia asked.

Neisei's face grew serious.

"It is one of the vilest words known to the history of Andez. There is no real translation into our tongue so I cannot tell you exactly what it means," Neisei said solemnly. "Just know that it is not something you should say around him, or any of the Tohari family."

Xia nodded.

"But *fadi*, why should Tohari be so impacted by the word? He is not an outside worlder."

Neisei was quiet.

"I do not know," he said softly. "But *quelpi* do not worry about it too much. Just work on your training."

Xia nodded, still confused. Neisei turned to leave but paused.

"It was kind of you to let Tohari-*kai* stay at his house."

Xia nodded.

"I believed that as well."

Neisei smiled faintly and walked out of the door. Xia looked after him for a second more.

But he was still crying, she thought closing her eyes. *Why was he crying?*

Third Sign

Jin tossed in his sleep. Sweat broke out across his forehead and he was panting. His eyes were shut tightly as if he were in pain. He muttered something in his sleep and thrashed around. Jin woke up clutching his chest, heaving. He rubbed his face tiredly and ran his fingers through his hair. He clutched a fistful and tugged slightly. Was he going to ever get to sleep?

Jin slowly got out of his bed and walked to the washroom. He had a horrible headache and needed relief. Jin turned on the light wincing slightly because of the brightness. His feet shuffled over to the sink and his hands reached to turn the water on. Jin looked down at his fingers and found them drenched in crimson. Jin groaned and quickly turned on the water. He stuck his head under the flowing water and relished in its coolness. Jin turned off the water and looked up to find crimson eyes staring back at him. He gasped and quickly turned away. The first night he saw them he had screamed. Now they were nothing but a fright he could not get rid of.

The throbbing in his chest continued and Jin rubbed it. For the past weeks, since he first saw the letter, things inside of him seemed to change. He could not sleep, he barely ate and every night he would dream of white wings drenched in blood and his hands in the midst of it all. Sometimes, Xia would be in his dreams but she would be far away, unable to provide him with any comfort. When Jin woke up this time the dream had almost been the same. This time pale white flesh and strands of blood red hair accompanied the red eyes. The worse part of it all was that when he awoke he was injured.

Jin felt a trickle of moisture run down his arm. He rolled up his sleeve and saw blood sliding down his arm. Jin removed his shirt and looked at his arm. A thin mark was oozing blood. It looked like a half moon with a squiggle at the end of it and a dot in the middle of it. Jin took a towel from the cupboard hole and started to wipe away the blood. Jin winced as the towel brushed over the cuts in his skin. He bandaged the fresh marks and looked at his arm. These new marks stretched all the way down his arm. The old ones covered his shoulder, then his forearm, and then met with the new marks. Jin let out a sad chuckle.

"What is happening to me?" he whispered to himself. Jin held his bandaged arm.

"That pull in my body won't stop... I ache everywhere and I... I can't go to sleep without being afraid I'm going to see that dream..."

Jin slowly got up from his sitting position and cleaned the mess he made. He had to tell his father and mother. This could not remain a secret forever. Jin turned off the light in the washroom and walked over to his father and mother's room. He opened the door and found them sleeping peacefully. Toi had his arms protectively around Are's waist and his head was resting on top of hers. Are nestled between her husband's arms and her head snuggled into his chest. Jin felt a pang of guilt for waking them up, but he was in distress.
Jin padded over to the side of his parents' bed.

"Dad, mom," he said softy, "please wake up."
The throbbing rang throughout his body and Jin winced.

"Dad! Mom!" Jin said louder which worked. Toi slowly opened his eyes and looked to the side. Once noticing Jin he turned to Are and shook her awake. It took more than one try to get her up, but once she was awakened she looked at Jin surprised.

"Jin what's wrong?" Are asked sitting up. Toi shifted besides her to look at his son as well.
Jin looked at his parents and wanted to say something but his throat would not open.

"Jin?" Toi asked quietly.

"...It hurts," Jin whispered quietly. "It hurts so much..."

Are quickly reached over Toi and took her son's hand. Somehow the pain ebbed and Jin felt comforted.

"Where?" she asked worried. "What's wrong?"

Jin slowly sat on the bed and closed his eyes.

"To tell you the truth, I feel so much better now that I'm with you so I'm trying to be strong," Jin whispered with a faint grin on his lips.

Are smiled and Toi took Jin's other hand.

"We're here for that reason," Toi said. "Parent's are *supposed* to make their children feel better."

Jin smiled faintly and silence filled the room. His parents looked at him expectantly.

"I wake up every night and a new mark is made," Jin said not knowing where to start. "Since you told me what that word meant I've been in pain... Geez... what's going on with me?"

Toi and Are exchanged a look and Are sighed.

"What do the markings look like?"

Jin shrugged.

"I've never seen them before," he replied. "Here... take a look for yourselves."

Jin held out his arm and Toi started to unwrap the bandages.

"You said you've been like this since I told you what the word meant, right?" Are asked. Jin nodded. "And you just decided to show us this now?"

Jin nodded.

"Yeah," Jin said. "I thought it would just go away... obviously I was wrong."

Toi smirked.

"Obviously."

One thing Jin loved about his parents was the fact that they never over did anything. Here he was about to show them strange cuts that seemed to enjoy marking his arm and they were making jokes on him. It made Jin feel like everything was going to come out fine in the end… *wherever* the end was.

Toi finished unwrapping the bandages and turned on the light. Jin watched his father's face for a reaction and all he received was an eyebrow raise. His mother gently let her fingers run over the marks.

"These look familiar…" Are said softly. "But I can't remember where from."
Toi nodded.

"Yes. These are strange. Certainly not from Hainai," he said. "It's remarkable that they just look like they've healed instead of looking like they were just made."

"Yes," Are said. "We have another project on our hands Toi-*pi*."

"Let me ask you Jin. When you receive these cuts do you see anything?" Toi asked.
Jin nodded.

"Yeah," he replied. "I usually see these eyes in the mirror- red and really frightening. I nearly wet myself the first time I saw them,"
Jin chuckled.

"And now?" Are asked. She had a smile on her face.

"Now I just get startled. I know they're going to be there but I can't help but jump," Jin replied. "Why aren't you guys freaked out by this?"
Toi shrugged.

"We're out in the outside world more then we are here. We see things that would kill most people on sight. You get used to it."

"So this is something common on the outside world?" Jin asked feeling slightly hopeful.
Are giggled.

"We didn't say that, Jin. We just said that we were not going to be 'freaked out' like you said," Are replied. Jin frowned. Even on the outside world this was not normal.

Are gently stroked her son's cheek. Toi started to put the bandages back on his arm.

"Don't worry Jin. We'll figure this out and you won't be in pain anymore."

Jin nodded. He held onto his mother's hand still feeling troubled.

"There is one thing I haven't told you guys yet…" Jin said softly.

Toi looked up from his work concerned.

"What? The scary person in the washroom mirror is attacking you?" he asked.

Jin laughed but quickly settled into his frown again.

"No… and yes," he replied. "I've been having these dreams that have been keeping me awake for weeks…"

Are gripped her son's hand.

"What about?" she inquired.

"…These wings are covered in blood… and hands- *my* hands are drenched in blood. I sometimes see Xia but she is too far away to do anything. And tonight, I saw those eyes with really pale skin…and red hair," Jin explained, "…and I have to admit, I'm scared."

Are nodded and leaned over to kiss her son on his head.

"Of course you're scared," she said gently. "You have such odd things happening to you and I'm pretty sure it has nothing to do with puberty."

Jin laughed and hugged his mother.

"Thanks," he said then gave his father a hug. "I feel so much better now."

Toi and Are nodded.

"Good," they said then looked at each other. They both cracked smiles and laughed. Jin loved his parents so much.

"Say Jin," Are said in an offhand manner.

"Yeah?"

"Do you have anyone else you feel...I don't know, *comforted* around besides us?"

Jin looked confused and thought for a moment. That time he read the letter and blanked out Jin woke up in Xia's arms. It was a very comforting position to be in. He blushed and his mother giggled excitedly. Toi smiled, amused at his wife's antics.

"Okay Are, I think Jin understands where you're getting at," Toi sighed. "Jin when we aren't here, we don't want you to be in pain. So please, whoever this person is, go to them."

"But what if the person doesn't want to comfort me?" Jin asked. *She might be changing but she hasn't changed yet.* Jin thought. *For all I know she could turn on me and kick me out in the cold.... Her parents might not though... they seem to like me.*
Are looked at Jin with soft eyes.

"Deep within every person's heart is the desire to comfort and be comforted. Let's just say it is especially potent in the heart of a woman," Are said. "I do not think you know anyone who will turn you out without a proper reason."
Jin nodded but was not quite sure.

"I'll just have to see."

*   *   *

Jin slapped the weapon out of Xia's hand with a roar. It clattered on the ground before disappearing. A victorious smirk graced his lips. Xia was on the ground holding her head in pain. She and Jin were sparring with one another in her snow-covered garden.

"I see *you're* feeling better," she huffed.
Jin grinned.

"So much better that I kicked your butt!" Jin laughed.
Xia smirked.

"Not quite."

The next thing he knew Jin was sprawled on the ground with a rod pointed at his neck.

"Not fair!" Jin cried angrily. "You cheated."

"No, you just were caught off guard," Xia replied. "So *I'm* victorious."

Jin scowled.

"I liked you better when you hated me."

Xia huffed again and puffs of hot breath came out her mouth.

"What makes you think I don't?" she questioned.

Jin stood up and dusted his backside off before it froze off.

"*'Why was he crying?'*" Jin grinned and mimicked Xia. "Your father so graciously told me that you were worried about me. Honestly, I'm flattered."

Xia's face turned red and Jin grinned.

"Don't be!" she stomped off deeper into the garden. Jin skipped after Xia.

"What? I can't feel happy that you were worried? We *are* partners after all!" Jin said skipping up to Xia.

"Please *don't* remind me," Xia muttered. Jin grinned and chuckled. He watched Xia walk in the snow ahead of him and sighed. Her cheeks and nose were rosy from the cold, but she looked as if she was not cold in the least. Her hair was tied back in a ponytail and large snowflakes were caught in it. She wore a black coat and Jin was surprised she could even fight in it. The dark color brought out her skin amazingly, but it was still a little too severe for her. Xia turned around and looked at Jin questioningly.

"Why are you staring at me like that?" she asked sourly.

Jin feigned hurt.

"You're acting like I'm doing something wrong," he said. "I'm only looking."

Xia whipped her head back around and started stomping again. Jin caught the blush on her cheeks.

"I'm not some doll to look at!" Xia snapped.
Jin laughed and tromped after her.

"You know… since I was lookin' and all," Jin started, "…why don't you wear another color besides black? I think they would compliment your skin better."
Xia turned to give Jin a sour look.

"What are you my stylist now?" she asked. "I'd rather not, thank-you."
Jin shrugged.

"Seriously though, try wearing a lighter color. Magenta might-"

"*Magenta*…?"
Xia gave Jin a 'you-are-positively-mad' look.

"Okay, maybe not magenta," Jin said quickly. "Red then."
Xia did not reply. Jin took that as an okay.

"Okay! We should go into the city sometime! I'd buy you some clothes," Jin said grinning.

Xia turned back around and walked some more. Jin rushed to catch up with her.

"What, you don't like that idea?"

"…Why can't *mothi* buy clothes for me?"

"Because she will buy what you ask her to buy. You say black and she'll buy black. Besides, you need to get out more. It'll be fun! I'll show you all the cool places to go shopping."

Xia was silent for a long time. Jin thought he said something to upset her and walked in front of her to look in her face. His face broke up in a grin. Xia was blushing furiously.

"…Is this like a date?" she questioned quietly. Jin smiled brightly and wiped away some snow that had fallen on her face. Her cheeks turned a darker shade of red.

"Only if you want it to be," he replied.

Xia turned away from Jin and walked towards the house.

"I… don't want it to be," she whispered.

Jin shrugged.

"Okay then," he said following her, "as friends then."

Xia paused.

"...Friends?"

Jin nodded.

"Yeah. We're at least that, right?"

Xia did not say anything for a moment.

"...At most."

Jin smirked.

"Of course, *bavdnah*."

Xia whirled around angry.

"Jin Tohari!"

Jin laughed and took off running. She was a very comfortable person to be with... even as she hit him over the head for being rude.

"I was joking, *bavdnah*! Ow! Really, *really* I was joking!" Jin cried.

"I am not your *bavdnah*! When will you understand?!" Xia yelled hitting Jin repeatedly on the head.

Jin finally flopped onto the snow-covered ground in defeat.

"You win... geez. Can't even take a joke."

Xia rolled her eyes.

"You just don't understand how much commitment it takes to be a *bavdnah*," Xia muttered. "It goes deeper than just the word lover. When someone is *bavdnah* it is the only commitment they are to have. The punishment for breaking *bavdnah* is severe."

Jin rolled over in the snow.

"I know that," Jin said smiling. "Why do you think I call you *bavdnah*?"

Xia blushed furiously.

"You don't get it at all!" she huffed and stormed in the direction of her house.

Jin lay still on the snowy ground watching the flakes float down to him. It set him at ease. He turned his head to the side and gazed at Xia's footprints.

"Why do you think I call you *bavdnah*?" he questioned softly. "It's because... I..."
Jin closed his eyes and rested in the snow.

"Tohari-*kai*! You're going to catch a cold!" Tudios called to him. Jin sat up and looked at the Chang residence. Tudios was waving for him to come back. Jin grinned and stood up. He ran to the house leaving a trail of footprints in his wake.

*　　*　　*

Xia could not stop the blush from rising to her cheeks when she thought of Jin. He made her feel things she thought were not real to her. She worried after him and looked out for him. She wanted to know if he was alright after the letter and if anything else upset him. She looked at him when he was not looking and could not stop looking. Her heart skipped a beat every time he was close enough to touch and it became hard for her to keep a straight face. Why did Jin make her so... not cool, not calm and not together? She could fall apart if he kept this up!

"*Why do you think I call you* bavdnah?" Jin's question ran through Xia's head. She groaned in frustration. Why did he make everything so difficult for her?

Xia walked to the door of the meditation room. Jin was waiting for her on the other side, not too patiently. He probably changed into something else and was ready to learn some other form of magics from her. Xia was not ready to deal with him so soon. "*Why do you think I call you* bavdnah?" His question floated into her head once more. Xia closed her eyes tightly willing for his words to go away.

"Are you finished yet? We have to go!" Jin's voice inquired through the door. Xia snapped out of her confused

114

state and growled angrily. She ripped open the door to a surprised Jin.

"Stop asking so many times already!"

Jin smirked.

"About time you heard me. We have to catch a train, so you better hurry up."

Xia looked confused.

"Where are we going?" she asked.

Jin knocked her head slightly.

"The city, stupid. You said you would come with me."

Xia stood in the doorway still confused.

"That is not today…"

"What better time than today?" Jin asked excitedly. "Knowing you, you would deny you said it and make me suffer."

Xia scowled.

"I wouldn't mind making you suffer," she muttered.

Jin laughed and grabbed Xia's hand. He pulled her towards the stairs.

"Wait Tohari! What about my parents? We have to ask them first!" Xia said quickly. Her heart was beating too fast for her comfort and she did not know what do while Jin was holding her hand.

"I already asked your dad and mom. They said it was a great idea."

Xia's eyes widened. Even her parents betrayed her!

"But… but…!"

Jin turned around and was face to face with Xia. He was very close to her. Very, *very* close…

"You don't have anymore excuses to make," Jin said. Xia did not want to think that his voice was lower than usual or that it held husky tones in it.

"So just come along for the ride."

Xia was trying to control the heat that came to her face. Why was this all happening to her now?

"You can turn the other way now..." she grumbled hoping it sounded annoyed.

Jin smirked.

"You know... I kind of *like* being this close...."

Xia leaned backwards to get away from Jin.

"Stop... leaning towards me!" Xia snapped.

Jin smirked.

"One little kiss will not kill you," Jin said.

Xia's eyes widened and her face flushed. He was joking... he was absolutely joking. Jin leaned in a little more.

He was absolutely serious! Xia was about to panic.

"Don't look at me like that!" Xia cried. "I will kill you Tohari!"

Jin chuckled and winked at Xia. Her heart rate slowed by a fraction.

"You don't actually expect me to kiss you when you're expecting it, do you?"

Xia felt herself nodding. Jin laughed.

"Well don't," he said. "I won't kiss you unless you're not expecting it."

Xia felt disappointed... and immediately crushed the feeling.

"Then what was the point of you scaring me like that?"

Jin laughed.

"I feel very... comfortable with you."

Xia's heart picked back up. *Oh no.* She thought. *He's going to say it...! What am I going to do? What do I say? Why am I so panicked?*

"I've been thinking about it for a while," Jin continued, "and I think that you're the only one who can help me get over this."

Xia opened her mouth and tried to say something understandable.

"Over what?" she managed.

Jin's lips curved in the softest smile Xia had ever seen and it made her heart stop. Could a person really have such an effect on another? Did Tohari really have to look that attractive right now?

"I'll tell you if I think we can conquer it together," he replied.

"You just said that I might be able to help you…" Xia countered confused.

"Yeah, I said it."

"You did not mean it?"

"I meant it."

"Then why are you going back on your word?"

"I'm not. I just think that you aren't ready to know about it yet."

"Why not, Tohari?"

"Because… you and I both know that you are not… there yet."

"Where yet?"

Jin lifted a finger to Xia's cheek and stroked it gently. She blushed.

"Do you even know why you are doing what you're doing?" Jin asked.

"What are you talking about?" Xia questioned very confused.

"Do you know why you're blushing?" Jin asked clearer this time.

Xia had no idea why she was blushing or why she liked the way Jin touched her face.

"…I want you to help me, but not until you understand what you are feeling," Jin explained.

"I know what I feel!" Xia said quickly.
Jin chuckled.

"No you don't," he said pinching Xia's cheek. She held it surprised.

"When I first met you, you had only one emotion and that was no emotion. How can I believe you when you say that you know what you feel, when it's only been a few months? I don't know how long it's been, but you haven't felt emotion in a long time."

"Tohari..."

Xia did not like it how Jin knew everything that was going on in her head and she knew nothing about what was going on in his.

"So, enough serious talk, Xia," Jin said grinning. "We're going to the city. Maybe you'll get some emotional experience when you get there."

"Maybe you will stop talking like you know everything!" Xia huffed. Jin grinned and continued down the stairs.

"That'll never happen," he said. Xia looked down at their fingers. He was still holding her hand.

*   *   *

Jin was right. Xia did gain some emotional experience, but not until she arrived back at her house. She walked into the door feeling confused but elated somehow. She had bags filled with clothes she thought she would never try on in her life and her head swam with thoughts about the evening. She tried to tell herself that they were friends- that she could not handle being more than that, but every time she did think about... being more than Jin's friend; butterflies would harass her stomach and blush would taint her cheeks. To make things harder for her, Jin decided to kiss her on her forehead before letting her into the house. And when she entered the house, her smile (her first real smile in a very long time), faded from her lips. Her father and mother's expressions were a mixture of sadness and seriousness. Xia did not like the feel of the sitting room when she walked into it.

"*Quelpi*, it is nice to see you home," Tudios smiled. Her daughter looked so alive and... normal. It saddened her to think that she and her husband would possibly shatter it.

"*Mothi*..." Xia acknowledged. "Is something wrong?"

"Ah, yes," Neisei said, "*quelpi* it seems you have received a letter from Bluse that you have not told us about."

"I have a letter but I have not yet opened it," Xia replied confused. "How did you know?"

"We just received a sphere from the Ludwig family. You know their son, Hans-*kai*, he works in the same field as you."

"I remember him," Xia muttered sourly. "He tried to convince the both of you that we were to be wed. Why do you have anything to do him?"

Neisei and Tudios did not reply.

"Is there some sort of problem?" Xia asked.

"Actually," Neisei said in a serious tone, "Hans-*kai* has informed us that, that letter you have failed to open is a warning. You have been put on trial and found guilty for treason."

Xia's bags dropped to the floor.

"What...?"

Tudios placed her hands to her mouth and looked away.

"We have not told you yet, *quelpi*, but... Tudios and I fear that this has to do with your prophecy," Neisei said with a pained look on his handsome face.

"...What are you talking about?" Xia asked. "Treason? Prophecy? What have I done wrong?"

Neisei held Tudios and looked at his daughter with a sad expression on his face.

"I fear that it is time you learn the truth."

Xia looked up at her parents with lost eyes. She was not ready for any of this.

Blood Prophecy

In a week's time, Jin's other arm became completely covered in markings. His body completely lacked energy to do anything and because he could not eat properly, his functions were shutting down completely. But that was not the worst part of it all. After the wonderful afternoon in the city was over, Xia sphered him with the bad news. She had been tried and found guilty for…treason?

Jin had never felt so angry in his life, but he was not angry with Xia. She did not know about it at all. He was angry just because he was angry. He was angry because he needed to feel justified in hating someone. How could her own organization *betray* her like that? Jin ground his teeth together when he thought of the pain Xia was going through.

Xia was sitting in his sitting room, sipping tea. She fashioned a red turtleneck and a pair of navy jeans, both compliments of her shopping trip with Jin. She was avoiding her house because she could not take the pressure she was being put under and she was convinced that her parents were going to betray her as well. Jin sat next to her with a cup of tea in his hands. Being with her like this made him feel so warm. They were not talking but the silence was comfortable. Jin could feel her eyeing him and grinned.

"Is there something you like?" Jin asked wagging his eyebrows suggestively.
Xia blushed.

"Don't flatter yourself," she muttered. Times like these made Jin feel very happy.

"I will, don't worry," Jin grinned. He took a sip of his sweet tea and the nostalgic feeling he usually felt did not wash over him. *Because I am already home,* Jin thought warmly.

"Say Tohari…" Xia's voice broke him out of his thoughts.

Jin looked at Xia.

"Yeah?"

"…How are you feeling?" Xia asked softly.

Jin closed his eyes and leaned back into his seat.

"Do you want the honest answer?" Jin asked.

Xia gazed up at him with worried eyes.

"Tohari?" she questioned

"I feel horrible," Jin replied. "Absolutely terrible."

"Oh…"

Jin and Xia remained in silence for a long time. Jin's body melted into the chair exhausted. Being with Xia made him so much better, but he was still in pain. Jin's eyes started to close.

"Tohari?" Xia broke the silence again.

"…Yes?" Jin asked opening his eyes.

Xia looked into her cup of tea.

"Never…mind."

Jin lifted his head and looked at Xia confused.

"What's wrong?" Jin asked.

Xia opened her mouth to reply, but Are walked in and Xia shut her mouth.

"Oh don't mind me. Just eavesdropping."

Jin and Xia both blushed.

"Mom!" Jin said embarrassed.

"Hello Xia-*pi*. How are you today?" Are asked ignoring her son.

"I am well. Thank-you," Xia replied. "And yourself?"

Are tittered.

"I'm fine. I see you two are making fast friends."

Xia smiled faintly.

"Your son is stubborn."

"I know. He takes after his father. Toi wouldn't leave me alone until I agreed to marry him."

"That is not how it went," Toi Tohari walked into the room.

Are looked at her husband questioningly, but a smirk was on her lips.

"How did it go then, *hanev?*"

Toi sat by his wife grinning.

"If I remember correctly, I took you away from your fiancé at the time because you *willingly* fell for me. It's not my fault I just happen to be perfect for you," Toi explained.

"Wait dad! You took mom's fiancé's place?" Jin asked excitedly.

Toi nodded.

"Something like that," Toi said. "Sometimes a man has to do things to save the people he loves. It may hurt them at first, but it usually comes out alright in the end."

Jin was amazed.

"Pardon, but how did you take Are-*ken*'s fiancé's place?" Xia asked. Jin could tell she was trying not to seem *too* interested.

Toi and Are exchanged a look and Are shrugged.

"Well, I beat him in a duel. He… still holds a grudge because of it," Toi said. "But I don't think people do that anymore."

"Do you know what they do now?" Jin asked.

Toi shook his head.

"You're the teen here, not me," he replied.

Jin chuckled.

"Are you sure? I think I act more like an adult than you do!" Jin said grinning.

Xia looked skeptical.

"I highly doubt that," she said.

Are smiled.

"I agree with Xia-*pi*," Are said. "Speaking of Xia-*pi*, how long do you plan on staying here?"

Jin and Xia exchanged a look.

"'I'm sure this whole problem with *quelpi* will ride over.' Is what Neisei-*pi* said to us," Are said smirking, "'until then please take care of her.' Is what your mother said to us."

Jin and Xia looked shocked. Toi laughed.

"Did you really think that we would not sphere your parents and inquire if they knew you were here or not?" Toi asked. "We have to know what our Jin is getting into nowadays."

"Are you mad at us?" Jin asked.

"Are we ever?" Toi replied. "We'll be here to help you with your problems, no matter what."

Jin felt so relieved that his parents were so flexible.

"Thanks," Jin said softly.

His parents smiled.

"Is there anything we could help you with?" Toi asked. "Anything you want to know?"

"...I do not think you will be able to help..." Xia said quietly.

"Don't be too sure," Jin started, "Dad and mom know lots of stuff from the outside world. Maybe they can help you."

Are looked at Toi and Toi shrugged.

"From what your parents have told us... there was a prophecy made when you were born. You know about that, right?" Are asked.

Xia nodded.

"Yes," she replied. "My father and mother told me about it a few days ago."

Toi looked concerned.

"You probably feel as if they should have told you earlier, yes?" Toi asked.

Xia nodded.

"They were not going to tell you until you were a few years older. I believe they thought that what they were doing was for the best. You still don't fully understand the weight of the prophecy," Toi explained.

"So you know what it is then?" Jin asked. "And you know why Bluse is accusing Xia of treason?"

Are nodded.

"We can put one and one together," she said.

"What do you mean?" Jin asked.

"The prophecy," Toi said. "Are-*pi*, do the honors, would you?"

Are gave her husband a bitter smile.

"You really are a horrible man," she said. "But Jin, the prophecy goes something like 'Crimson eyed angel from the higher skies joins the lost princess of war, bonded o'er the clouded body of the host'."

Jin stared at his parents with a blank face.

"It means Tohari, that an Andez is going to join a Bluse," Xia said.

Are nodded.

"Almost, but you've missed an important detail," Are said. "The Andez is not going to be normal. What I mean to say is that the Andez will need to break free of a host in order to fully join the Bluse."

Jin's eyes widened.

"So you mean… the Andez is *using* someone as a host?" he questioned incredulously.

Are nodded.

"What will happen once the Andez breaks free?" Jin asked slowly.

Toi looked almost… burdened.

"The host will disappear."

Xia gasped.

"Because of me?" she whispered shocked.

Jin turned to her confused.

"What do you mean?"

"The reason we started this whole conversation was because of me," Xia snapped. "The prophecy was *my* prophecy… now I understand."

"*I* don't," Jin muttered. "Can someone explain it to me."

"Xia-*pi* is the reason for the Andez's return, Xia-*pi*'s presence is necessary. What she understands is that she has been in the constant presence of the Andez's host and because of that the Andez is awakening," Toi explained.

"Oh," was all Jin could say. There was a long silence in the room before Are decided to speak.

"Why don't you show Xia to her room?" Are suggested.

Jin nodded and Xia stood up.

"Thank-you for explaining everything to me and for letting me stay here."

"Thanks for being here," Are said. "We love having you."

Jin and Xia left the sitting room and Are placed her head on Toi's shoulder tiredly.

"Those two…" she sighed.

Toi gently rubbed his wife's back.

"Do you want to give me a massage?" Are asked her husband. Her voice begged him.

"Ah, do I have a choice?"

Are turned her back to Toi and he started to knead into her shoulders. Toi chuckled when his wife let out a little sigh of pleasure.

"You're all tense," Toi noticed in a second's time. "Let me get the knots out for you."

Are smiled.

"You've gotten amazingly skilled at the language of touch," she said. "I'm very impressed."

"Practice makes perfect."

Are giggled and pressed her back into Toi's hands. She fell into his chest once his fingers gently relinquished their hold on her back.

"Are you alright?" he asked her softly.

Are slid her hands up Toi's arms and released a sigh. Her fingers slid into his hair and he pulled her close.

"Are you really this stressed?" Toi asked once his arms were securely wrapped around his wife's waist.

"I am," she replied.

"Because of Cayn?"

Are nodded.

"Both of Jin's arms are marked. Do you think we will be able to tell him now?"

"What the markings mean, you mean?"

Are nodded.

"Yes."

"Is it almost time?"

"Yes."

"So that means Jin will disappear soon?"

"…Yes."

Toi held onto Are tightly.

"It has to be this way. It's in the prophecy."

Are nodded and a tear fell from her eye. Toi wiped it away tenderly and kissed her neck.

"In order for us to secure Jin's and Cayn's happiness, the prophecy must be fulfilled. In order for it to be fulfilled no obstacles can be in the way. In order for that to happen you have to be strong."

"…You know how to make me feel better," Are said bitterly. "Can I wallow in sorrow for a moment? I am putting Jin through all this pain."

"So am I," Toi said. "When we took our hair down, it meant that we would do anything for the child to succeed. It meant taking these forms, it meant hiding, it meant hurting your child to have him live."

"Toi…"

"When you were with child, Are, I told myself that no matter what I would see to it that the prophecy was fulfilled but more than that, I told myself that I would be there to support you when it happened."

Are closed her eyes against the tears that were threatening to spill.

"I see…" she said.

Toi pressed his lips to Are's neck again.

"I'm glad you do because Jin is going to need all the support he can get."

Jin settled Xia into the guest bedroom. He placed all of her things next to the drawers so she could put them away when she pleased. After he finished, Jin stood around the room almost nervous. Xia sat on the bed fingering the comforter and looking anywhere but at Jin.

"So... how do you like it?" Jin asked after a minute.

"I like it very much," Xia replied.

Jin grinned.

"I'm glad. I mean it isn't as large as your house but-"

"I think it is very comfortable," Xia said cutting Jin off. "Thank-you."

Jin nodded and looked for someplace to sit. He sat at the desk and looked back at Xia. She was staring at him.

"What?" he asked.

Xia shrugged.

"You seem nervous," she replied simply. "I think I am too."

"Why?" Jin asked.

"I don't really know. But I've been feeling like this for a while around you..."

Xia's hand flew to her mouth in surprise. Jin grinned. *Probably didn't even realize it was coming out,* Jin thought. *She's cute.*

"Don't worry. I won't hold it against you," Jin said grinning. "I like you."

Xia blushed and Jin laughed. Silence filled the room.

"R-really?" she asked shyly. It was the first time Jin heard her stammer.

"I'm being completely honest," Jin said. "I like you a lot more now because I can actually see what you're feeling."

"Tohari..."

Jin held up his hands in surrender.

"Don't worry. I'm not going to pounce or anything," Jin said. "I just felt like getting it off my chest."

"How can you just say it so freely?" Xia asked looking away. Her face was still red.

Jin shrugged.

"I don't know. I always thought it would be hard, but here I am telling you how I feel. Being friends first really helps," Jin said grinning.

"Friends huh," Xia started, "…I've never felt the need to have friends."

"Because you cannot relate to people here," Jin said. "I've always been fascinated by the outside world and to me you were just as interesting. So I wanted to find out everything about you. I'm sorry about being a little pushy in the beginning."
Xia nodded.

"I am fine with it now I guess," Xia said. She blushed. "I don't know how to say this but… I am confused by you."
Jin tilted his head in question.

"How?"

"You say things that just… I do not know what to do when you say them. And then you hold onto me and touch me and I just do not understand why my face flushes when I think of you. Could I be growing in affection for you or… I just can't figure myself out," Xia replied and looked up at Jin. "Why are you looking at me like that?"

Jin had a grin on his face but his eyes were sympathetic.

"You're crying."

"I am," Xia touched her cheek and felt the wetness on her fingers, "… not."

Jin walked over to Xia and chuckled. He rubbed the tears away but more kept coming.

"Why am I crying?" Xia asked herself and she tried to wipe them away.

Jin tenderly rubbed Xia's cheek and she looked into his eyes.

"It's not a bad thing to cry," Jin said softly. Xia's face scrunched up and she let out a sob. Jin smiled and encircled her in his arms.

"You don't cry!" Xia muttered into Jin's chest.

Jin rubbed her back slowly.

"Sure I do," he said. "Everyone has to cry."

"*I* don't!"

"Aren't you right now?"

"No! Something's in my eye."

"And making your nose run."

Xia banged her fist against Jin who winced.

"I hate you! This is all your fault."

Jin lifted Xia's head to look into her eyes.

"I'll let it be my fault if you shut-up and cry."

"I hate you…!"

Xia buried her head in Jin's shoulder and cried some more.

"Why do you think it happened?" Xia asked after she calmed down and changed.

"You're probably frustrated and all of your frustration just popped," Jin replied. "It happens to people like you who don't show their emotions all the time."

"What do you mean?"

"It's called a break down. Every normal person has one sometime in their lifetime."

"What happened when you had one?"

Jin sighed deeply.

"…I haven't had one yet."

Xia looked at Jin questioningly.

"Why haven't you had one yet?"

Jin shrugged.

"I don't know. I guess I'm not ready to have one yet."

Xia placed a hand on top of Jin's hair and grinned.

"Well when you need to cry, you can lean on my shoulder."

Jin smirked.

"I have already haven't I?"

Xia blushed.

"That doesn't count as a break down," Xia muttered. "I don't know what that counts as."

Jin sat up and ran his fingers though his hair.

"Neither do I," he said softly.

Xia looked up at him, silent.

"I can't remember what happened," Jin started, "I can't remember anything at all."

"Nothing?" Xia inquired.

Jin shook his head.

"I remember reading the letter and then feeling pain..." Jin rubbed his chest although it did not hurt very much. "After that I woke up clinging onto you and I felt so much better."

"You do not know what you did?"

Jin shook his head.

"You went mad," Xia replied. "You took the letter and burned it. Then you turned towards me and your eyes were red-"

"My eyes were what?" Jin asked quickly. Xia was startled.

"Red?" she asked confused.

Jin whimpered and rested his head in his hands.

"What's wrong?" Xia asked quickly.

Jin rubbed his face again, determined not to think about the eyes.

"My eyes were red...?"

"Tohari? Are you alright?"

Jin sighed and rested his eyes on Xia.

"I have something to show you... something you will find a little scary."

Xia looked confused.

"What are you talking about?"

"Remember the thing I told you about at your house? The thing that you can help me out with?"

Xia nodded still confused.

"Well I'm about to show it to you."

"Are you sure I'm ready?"

Jin grinned.

"Perfectly ready."

Jin fingered the hem of his shirt and started to lift it over his head.

"What are you doing?!" Xia cried alarmed.

Jin smirked.

"I'll only strip when we're married," Jin said with amusement in his voice.

"Don't... flatter yourself."

Jin grinned and with one fluid movement stripped the shirt off his body. Xia gasped. Jin's arms were covered in thin markings as red as blood.

"What... are they?" Xia asked shock ridden all over her face. "How long have they been there Tohari?"

"I don't know what they are," Jin replied, "and they've been there since I saw what the letter said. Every night, after that incident a new mark cuts into my skin."

"Did it hurt?"

"Naturally."

Xia looked like she was about to cry and Jin had no idea why.

"Woah, what's wrong?" Jin asked quickly. "I know it's ugly but they're on me."

"I could not do anything to stop this..."

Jin breathed a sigh of relief. Was that all?

"You didn't know about it so how could you have done something?"

Xia gently touched one of the cuts with her finger.

"How can I help you now? It's already done."

Jin laughed a hallow laugh.

"All I want you to do for me is hold on tight and never let me go," Jin said and plopped his head in the crook of Xia's neck.

"Tohari!"

"When I'm with you like this, it doesn't hurt at all," Jin said quietly. "If you're near, I can bear the pain."

"Does it hurt a lot?" Xia asked.

Jin's hands fisted Xia's sweater and his head nodded.

"So, so much," he replied. Xia's arms wrapped around Jin's shoulders and held him to her.

"You idiot," she whispered, "you should know better than to try and do things on your own."

Jin chuckled.

"You know this means you can never let me go, right?"

Xia nodded.

"Don't flatter yourself," she said softly.

"I will."

*　　*　　*

Toi and Are woke up to a delicious aroma. Are sat up first and looked around groggily. Toi looked up at her and chuckled. Are looked down at her husband curiously and hopped out of the bed.

"Slow down Are," Toi said slowly getting out of the bed, "the food isn't goin' anywhere."

"How do you know? *Your* son eats like a horse."

Toi smiled, amused by his wife's antics.

"*My* son is he now?" Toi asked. "I always thought it took two people to make a child."

Are smirked.

"It took one person, one half person and a lot more stubbornness to make that child," she said.

Toi stretched and looked lovingly at his wife.

"I'm getting up, don't worry."

Toi finally managed to get out of bed and his wife led him down the stairs and into the kitchen. Xia was in the kitchen making breakfast with Aya and Jin. They looked like a family smiling together, laughing together, making *breakfast* together. Are was so happy she wanted to cry.

"Xia-*pi* you don't have to make breakfast," Are said walking over to the stove.

Xia nodded.

"It is fine," she said. "Aya was nice enough to want to help."

"What about me?" Jin questioned.

"What *about* you?" Xia asked.

Aya poked her brother in the side.

"Jin didn't wanna get outta the bed to help!" she said pouting.

Jin feigned hurt.

"Ow, Aya, betrayed by my own sister."

Aya giggled and continued to stir what smelled like blueberry pancakes. Jin kissed his sister softly on her head and turned to Xia.

"Need help?" he asked.

"Not from you," Xia replied smirking.

"What about you not letting me go?"

"It does not hurt now does it? You'll be fine."

Toi and Are smirked at Jin and Xia.

"They remind me of us," Are said softly. "When we were first married."

Toi nodded and held his wife close.

"With the exception that they're actually getting work done," Toi said grinning. "We didn't really get the chance to eat breakfast."

Are tittered softly.

"Yeah… we should do that again, sometime."

Toi laughed.

"…Sure."

"Old people, get a room!"

Toi and Are turned toward Jin.

"When you're older, you'll understand what *hanev really* means."

Jin blushed embarrassed and turned away.

My parents…geez, he thought.

Cayn's Desire

Xia opened the door to the bedroom to find a flower lying on her bed. The rose was strangely colored and Xia noticed it was larger than the ones in her garden. She stepped to her bed and picked the flower up. The bottom of the rose was pink, but it darkened at the tips becoming red. Xia closed her eyes and sniffed the flower. It had a very clean and warm scent. A note was attached to it and Xia smiled faintly when she read who sent it to her.

You are an idiot Jin Tohari, Xia thought smiling. He was trying to tell her he was okay. Xia placed the rose back on her bed and left her room to find a vase. She walked into the kitchen and opened a cabinet. She pulled out a small glass vase and filled it with water.

"*Quelpi* what are you doing?" Xia heard her mother's voice. She turned around with the vase in front of her.

"Tohari gave me a flower," Xia replied. "I wanted to put it in water."

Tudios Chang smiled warmly at her daughter.

"You are becoming more than friends then?" she asked.

Xia felt the laughter come up to her throat and released it. It was so strange to hear herself make such a happy noise.

"No, I do not think that will happen," Xia said. "Tohari's being himself is all."

Tudios nodded smiling.

"It's called sincerity," Tudios said in her soft voice. "Tohari-*kai* is showing you that he cares."

Xia looked at the water swaying in the small vase.

"He should not. Nothing good will come out of it." Xia said. "Nothing good at all…"

Tudios looked sympathetic for a moment, then tittered.

"I daresay something good has come out of it," Tudios whispered. "You are happy with him."

Xia blushed.

"You are reading too much into this *mothi*," Xia said. Her heart picked up every time her mother and father talked about Jin as if he were their son-in-law. Xia quickly made her way up the stairs to spare herself any more embarrassment. She made it to her haven and sighed. *That is the problem with these stupid emotions. You cannot just pick and choose which ones you want,* Xia thought bitterly. She would have very much liked not to have embarrassment as a feeling. It was too much of a pain.

Xia made her way to her bed again and placed the rose in the vase. She held it for a moment, looking for a place to put it. Xia moved the books over on the windowsill and placed the vase with the rose on top of it. The orange sunlight lit the petals on fire. Xia gently stroked the velvety flower petals. Her mind started drifting; thinking about Jin and why he sent her the flower in the first place.

Xia's hair splashed across the pillows when she flopped onto her bed. She could not help but think about when she first met Jin on a chase; and how they ended up the way they were now. A tear rolled down her cheek and Xia wiped it away. The image of Jin's shocked face popped into her head. There was no way either of them knew. For so long, Jin had been suffering and she could do nothing about it because she caused it. The reason she could make him feel better was because she was the only one who was the catalyst.

Xia turned her head to face the rose. Was he really alright? Would he ever be? Xia touched her arms. Jin had scars for the rest of his life because of her. Xia traced the scars on her own arms. The prophecy was forever etched into his flesh. Xia let out a small moan of frustration.

"Why was I so stupid?" she asked herself. "I *knew* it was outer world language! Why did I not just put it together?"

Xia closed her eyes and felt another tear trickle down her cheek. *'Stop beating yourself up!' Is what he'd tell me,* Xia thought. *'It's on me, not you. So stop.'*

"I cannot stop…" Xia muttered angrily. "It's *your* fault I cannot…"

"Is it really my fault?"

Xia shot up and glared in the direction of the voice. Jin Tohari was standing in the doorway, smirking like usual.

"I think you're just too shy to admit you *like* me," Jin said grinning. "But that's okay. I'll suffice on your hints."

Xia's eye twitched in annoyance, but she was blushing.

"What hints?" she questioned. "I do not drop hints."

Jin raised an eyebrow in a suggestive manner.

"Shut-up Tohari!" Xia snapped.

"I didn't *say* anything," Jin said innocently. "I came here to cheer you up, like a good friend and all I get is a 'shut-up Tohari'. I understand though. You'll tell me soon enough."

"Don't push your luck…"

Jin smirked and walked around Xia's bedroom. He examined the books on the shelf and walked over to the desk and chair.

"Who let you in?" Xia asked after a few seconds of watching Jin walk around her room.

"Your father. He says that it was fortunate that I stop by. You were bound to be miserable in your room by yourself," Jin replied. "And he was right."

Xia scowled but did not say anything else. Jin made his way to the windowsill and looked down at the flower in the vase.

"I'm glad you like it," Jin said quietly. "Aya and I were in town looking around for some stuff and she wanted to buy flowers for you. She said that they would make you feel better."

"I felt fine when I was in your home," Xia said surprised.

"Did you?" Jin asked. He tenderly fingered the petals that bathed in the warm light.

Xia held a confused expression on her face.

"Aya," Jin started, "has this thing when it comes to feelings. I know she's only five an' all, but she can tell when someone isn't feeling well. Not like sick, but more like unhappy and stuff like that."

"Oh," Xia said.

"Anyway, Aya and I went into the flower shop and started looking at all the flowers they had. Aya started asking me if the colors had meanings and stuff. I told her they did only if she believed they did and then I told her what they meant-"

"You knew them all?"

"I'm a guy," Jin replied grinning. "I only know the ones that count."

Xia rolled her eyes and Jin continued.

"So I told her about the meanings and we looked for a good one to give to you. Aya was convinced that I should give you a red one and I told her that I didn't think you were ready for that one yet."

"Why not?"

Jin grinned slyly.

"You mean you don't know? You call yourself Black Rose and you really don't know what they mean?" Jin taunted. Xia looked like she was about to kill Jin.

"Things like that do not matter in the outer world!" Xia muttered.

"Oh? I actually heard once that things like that *do* matter. Maybe you're just out of touch."

Xia huffed and looked away.

"Continue your story," she said angrily.

Jin smirked once more and continued.

"So like I was saying, red means love," Jin said to Xia's surprised face.

"But there's red on the rose now," she said confused. She looked at her flower and then at Jin. He was smiling at her with such warmth that it made her flush. He ran his fingers though his spiky black hair and chuckled. Xia wished she did not think he looked so handsome.

"You're skipping ahead," Jin said. "Hopefully for the last time, Aya went off into the store looking at the different flowers and I followed her at a distance. We came to the rose section and Aya insisted that I pick out one from here. Roses are her favorite flower, so I browsed through the section to give to you. I didn't want to be too cliché, but I enjoy making my sister happy."

I know, Xia thought fondly.

"*Anyway,* I found the most beautiful white rose. It was full and clean- the most perfect flower I've seen. I went to pick it up, and someone snatched it right from under me. So obviously that wasn't the one I was going to give to you. But right under that one was a multi-colored one. Pink and red. I thought it was perfect."

"So you bought it for me," Xia concluded. She wanted her heart to stop beating so quickly, but it was not listening to her. She was flattered.

"Actually, I bought a *dozen* for you, but I wasn't sure how you'd take it."

Xia's eyes became wide and she flushed scarlet. A dozen? *A dozen roses?* Jin was correct in thinking that she did not know how to react.

"Why would you... do that?" Xia asked unable to keep her embarrassment from showing before. Jin walked over to Xia and placed a hand on her head. She looked up to find him blushing slightly.

"I've told you before, I *like* you," Jin replied. "That's why I would do it."

Xia's heart definitely would give out soon if it did not stop beating the way it did.

"Besides," Jin fell backwards onto the bed, "I don't think I'll be able to spoil you when I disappear."

Xia felt her heart plummet. She closed her eyes and placed a hand over her heart to stop the ache.

"Don't say that..." she said quietly. "We'll find a way to make you *not* disappear."

Jin chuckled darkly.

"There is no way, *hanev*," Jin said with a sad smile on his face. "Even as we sit together now, he is taking over. You know you accelerate the process."

Xia jumped.

"Then get out! Get away quickly!" Xia said panicked.

Jin turned to look at Xia. He lifted his hand to her cheek and held it tenderly.

"*I* want to be here," Jin said firmly. "We both do, so don't kick us out."

Xia really wished Jin did not look so attractive.

"But... what if you disappear right now? I won't be able to see you again..." Xia whispered.

"Would it really be so bad, since you don't really like me?"

"But we are friends."

"Are we?"

"Are we not?"

Jin smirked.

"You're getting better at this."

Xia nodded with a small smile on her face.

"I know."

Jin let go of Xia's cheek and sat up.

"You know, I'm not going to disappear right now. So don't look at me like that."

"Like what?"

Jin grinned and looked at Xia with a tender expression. It was an expression Xia liked on Jin, but was very wary of.

"Like I'm about to disappear," Jin replied.

Xia lifted her hand to her cheek. She did not even know there was an expression for something like that.

"I do not look like that..." Xia said quietly but she really did not know what she looked like at all. Jin laughed.

"Yes you do," Jin said. "It's written all over your face. But don't worry; I'm not going anywhere yet."

Xia nodded and placed her hand back in her lap. Her eyes trailed to the rose on her windowsill and then back to Jin.

"Are you sure you're alright?"

Jin nodded, smiling faintly.

"I am," he said. "To tell you the truth, I thought my life was going to end right there, you know? I mean, in all the movies and stuff when the hero finds out something major it happens so suddenly."

Jin nodded again at an unseen question to Xia.

"So I'm grateful," Jin said. "I'm here for a few more months if I'm lucky."

"Tohari...?"

"*Hanev?*" Jin replied. Xia did not even blush this time.

"Does it hurt?" Xia asked.

Jin shook his head.

"No. I mean you're next to me so I can't feel the pain."

"What about when I'm not near you?" Xia asked.

Jin lifted his hand in the air and waved it around. Xia's eyes caught sight of the thin string around his ring finger. It used to be her hair tie.

"Remember when you gave this to me?" Jin asked. "It smells like you even though it is so small. It quells him so the pain is less."

Xia nodded, blushing slightly.

"I can give you a bigger one if you'd like," she said getting up from her bed.

Jin smiled and lifted the makeshift ring to his face.

"This one is just fine," Jin said.

Xia stared at Jin for a moment. His hair made spikes of their own accord and they fell into his face, framing it almost too perfectly. His honey colored eyes looked distant as they focused on her hair tie ring. He had a very attractive face, Xia hated to admit, and was a very nice height. He was not shorter than she was, but he was not tall enough to escape her wrath.

"See something you like?" Jin asked.

Xia was jolted from her stare.

"No," she snapped.

Jin laughed and got up from his position on the bed.

"I can't wait for the day when you come to me and say, *Jin you were right! I love you too!*"

"That will never happen," Xia muttered but her heart beat madly at Jin's words.

Jin shrugged.

"Sure it will. You said you'd never get caught but I caught you, right?" Jin said grinning. "But I won't rush you yet."

Xia glared and Jin laughed. There was a knock on the door and it opened. Tudios walked into the room with a tray filled with tea and cake.

"*Quelpi*, Jin-*kai* I thought you might like some tea and cake," Tudios said walking into the room.

"Thanks," Jin said grinning. Tudios handed him a cup and placed the cake on the bedside table.

"How are you today?" Tudios asked.

"I'm feeling well," Jin replied. "The shock has worn off."

Tudios nodded smiling faintly.

"I can see that very well. The roses you bought are lovely," Tudios said. "I hope *quelpi* has thanked you properly."

Jin nodded.

"She will," he said smiling. Tudios tittered and Jin laughed. Xia felt a little confused.

"I am glad," Tudios said. "If you need anything, let Neisei and I know."

Jin nodded.

"No problem," Jin grinned.

Tudios turned to Xia and smiled warmly.

"You look very happy right now," she said smiling. "Your father and I are glad."

Xia tilted her head in confusion when her mother turned to leave. Tudios closed the door behind her.

"What did she mean?" Xia asked.

Jin took a sip of his tea.

"You look happy," he said. "It's really self-explanatory."

141

Xia pouted and took up her teacup.

"Well maybe not to me," she snapped.

Jin chuckled.

"I'm sorry. I'll be more sensitive," Jin said.

Xia huffed and took a sip of her tea. The silence in the room made Xia feel uncomfortable, but she did not know what to say. She decided that she would not say anything at all. It would end up sounding out of place anyway.

"I'm glad your mother and father are pleased," Jin said softly. Xia looked over at him.

"Why?" she asked.

"Because when I go at least I know that I made your parents happy," Jin replied.

"Tohari... why are you talking like this?" Xia asked. "I do not think it will bring on anything good."

Jin looked into his teacup.

"Shouldn't we talk about it though? You can't avoid it anymore! I am the *host*. There is nothing that is going to change that," Jin said. "I want to be able to tell you what is happening to me and what he says..."

Xia pouted hurt.

"I do not care what he says!" Xia cried. "It's *his* fault you are going to disappear!"

A pained expression flashed across Jin's face and his hand flew to his heart.

"Are you alright?" Xia asked panicked.

"Please don't say things like that," Jin said in raspy tones. "You don't just hurt me."

Xia opened her mouth to argue but Jin placed a finger to her lips.

"Cayn is not your enemy Xia. It is not his fault he has a host. He had to be hid, just like you," Jin said. "I'm not going into the whole story but you're in Hainai because Bluse did not want you to find me and make the prophecy come true. That is why you never knew about it."

"I know that…" Xia said looking away. "Cayn-*kai* is not you and I just…"

Jin grinned and held one of Xia's hands.

"He'll grow on you. Just like I did," Jin said tenderly. He pulled Xia into an embrace and she flushed. She tried to get away and Jin tightened his hold.

"Stop moving, I'm trying to show you something," Jin said.

Xia's heart was beating too quickly and Jin was too close.

"*Honestly,* if I wanted to pounce I would've done it already," Jin muttered. "Just relax *hanev.*"

"How am I supposed to relax when you call me *bavdnah* and mean it?" Xia questioned flushed and angry.

Jin laughed.

"Like I said, if I were really going to kiss you I would have done it already," Jin said amusedly. "Now if you don't stay still I might have second thoughts."

Xia was redder than a tomato but was not about to risk getting kissed.

"And here I was hoping you'd let me," Jin said feigning hurt.

"Just show me what you wanted to and hurry up," Xia grumbled.

Jin nodded and closed his eyes.

"Now, relax," he said.

Xia did what she was told. Jin was a very persuasive person.

"Listen, do you hear that?" Jin asked.

Xia was quiet for a moment. She heard Jin's heartbeat and then something else. She inhaled sharply.

"Two heartbeats!" she gasped. "You have two heartbeats!"

Jin nodded and Xia looked at him for a second, then slammed her ear back to his chest.

"Geez can you be a little more gentle? But yeah, I have two heartbeats," Jin said. "One is mine and one is Cayn's."

Xia was amazed. There were definitely two heartbeats going on in his chest. Xia closed her eyes and listened for a long time. Jin placed his hand to her head feeling contented. After a while, Xia spoke in a soft voice.

"What is he like? What does he say to you?"

Jin closed his eyes again.

"He is a lot like how you were, to tell you the truth," Jin replied. "He is quiet and brooding but when he does talk he is... sincere."

"What does he look like?"

Jin shrugged.

"I wish I knew. When I look in the mirror I see myself," Jin replied softly. "But those few times... when the prophecy was being written onto my arms, I saw him, I think."

"What did you see?"

"Red eyes... red hair... and something white," Jin replied thoughtfully, "probably wings."

"...What does he say to you?"

Jin smiled.

"Many things," he said. "He wishes for the prophecy's fulfillment."

"That we will join?" Xia asked bitterly She lifted her head from Jin's chest.

"That you will be *hanev*," Jin replied smiling a joyful smile. Xia did not know why he grinned in such a happy way, but it brought butterflies to her stomach.

Jin's Requiem

"Say Xia?" Jin asked as he walked home from school with Xia.

"Yes?" she replied.

"What about those assassins that are after you because of the prophecy? Have they bothered you yet?"

Xia shook her head.

"No, not yet," she said. "I feel them though. So I think they are close but I cannot say for sure when they will attack me."

"Us."

"Me."

Jin sighed.

"You're impossible."

"I know."

Jin and Xia continued to walk down the street to the Chang residence in silence. Jin looked around Hainai and felt as if this would be one of the last times he would be able to enjoy its quiet. Jin grinned. He never liked quiet anyway. Suddenly, a loud explosion knocked Jin off his feet.

"Run, you twit!"

Jin Tohari looked to his side and saw Xia Chang dart into an alley. Jin's heart was hammering as he followed Xia into the alley. *Okay, so I don't like quiet, but I didn't ask for this!* Jin thought. All of a sudden, Xia jumped to the side of the alleyway and in her place was a sword sticking up from the ground. Jin looked at it but it did not register in his mind that it came from above until Xia told him to run again.

"What the heck is going on?!" Jin shouted.

Xia closed her eyes and put on her mask. The light that came from her blinded Jin.

"Why are you bothering with the mask now? They already know who you are!" Jin said staring at Xia as if she were crazy.

Black Rose glared, but kept a calm voice.

"Those assassins I told you about are here," Black Rose replied coolly. "I would prefer if you did not follow me anymore."

"Why? I'm here to help you!" Jin said. "We're partners!"

"This isn't some little game now!" Black Rose yelled. "They will not hesitate to kill you."

Jin smirked.

"I don't think you have to worry. You take care of yourself and I'll take care of myself."

Black Rose lifted her hand to touch Jin's cheek. His eyes widened slightly.

"If you die, I'll never forgive you. I'll never ever forgive you,"

Jin smiled and closed Black Rose's fingers within his own.

"Same thing goes for you," Jin said softly. He could not help but relish in the warmth of Black Rose's fingers. Would he be able to stay with her like this forever? There was a tingle in the back of Jin's head and it worried him. He grabbed Black Rose's waist and lunged forward. A loud banging noise made Jin's ears ring. He looked back to see a sword standing right where he had been.

"I'm sorry, did I interrupt your little moment?" a girlish giggle came from above them.

Black Rose glared and looked up at the person standing on the building.

"Lani!" Black Rose growled. "What the heck are you doing here?"

The girl on the roof, Lani, giggled again and jumped from the building and landed in front of Black Rose. She wore shiny red boots, a green jumper and a red tee shirt underneath. She tied her hair into curly ponytails on top of her head. She held a grin that was menacing.

"Here I am in town an' I get a message from the boss-says I have to get rid of you. Sorry hun."

Black Rose stood up, looking furious. Jin took a step back not willing to get in her way, yet. Jin felt the tingle again but it was not alarming. It seemed like it was cautious. Jin turned around looking into the dark alley. He had this horrible feeling... Jin took a shaky step forward. He tried to remember to be vigilant.

"You *would* like to get rid of me wouldn't you?" Black Rose said angrily. "You've always been trying to compete with me."

Lani smirked and materialized a sword.

"That's right eva' since Academy," Lani said in a sing-song voice. "Lil' Miss Prophecy always doing better tha' the rest of us- *thinking* she was better tha' the rest of us. Who would've thought, I would be the one sent to kiss ya good-bye?"

Black Rose readied herself and materialized a rod out of her magics.

"I will not be saying goodbye to anyone," Black Rose said. "Especially not to a jealous, second-class student."

Lani growled.

"Ya won't be sayin' that once you're dead!" She charged at Black Rose.

Black Rose jumped back, to avoid getting hit and lurched forward. She struck Lani to the ground.

"I doubt I will be able to say anything at all if that were the case."

Jin had wandered away from Black Rose in order to give her space and because the tingle in his head became more than a little caution sign. As he moved deeper into the alley-way, the tingle became stronger and his senses started to go crazy. Every little thing made his heart skip a beat or his body jump. Jin stopped walking for a moment. Someone... was behind him.

There was no movement, no sounds could be heard, but Jin could feel the presence of another body. He did not want to turn around unprepared. That was how heroes met their ends.

Jin noticed a garbage can lid close enough to reach. The tingle in the back of his head became stronger and Jin jumped forward, grabbed the trash lid and whipped around in time to block an attack aimed for his head. He gritted his teeth and jumped back.

"Who're you?" Jin yelled as he skid to a halt.

The man that attacked Jin wore a pair of black pants and a white sleeveless shirt. A black blindfold covered his eyes and dove into his short white hair. He looked not much older than Jin. He had two large swords in his hands that he swung around freely. Jin eyed the weapons wearily.

"I am Raifelle," the young man replied.

Jin eyed the man sourly.

"I don't care what Organization you're in! I want your name."

"Why? What good is a name to a person who is going to die?"

Jin did not like the young man in front of him, in the least. It was not because he was trying to kill him; it was because he did not answer questions in a way he could understand. The man took a step forward swinging his weapon wildly. Jin could only avoid getting hit by jumping backwards.

"Watch where you're swinging those things!" Jin yelled avoiding the blades right before they hit him.

"It is useless to try and run away. Your end is inevitable."

Jin materialized a sword and flung it between the two moving blades. The man caught Jin's sword between his two, but paused in his walking. Jin took the opportunity and pushed the man aside. A pang of guilt went through Jin. *Geez what have I gotten into? Pushing around blind people.* Jin thought.

He let out a startled yell as the man came from nowhere and landed in front of him. *Blind as I am*, Jin thought bitterly.

"You are pretty good, Andez," the young man said. "I should have not taken you lightly."

Wait, Andez? Jin thought. *I thought only their own kind called themselves that.* The young man reached for his blindfold and started tugging it off.

"Hey-hey! Why are you taking it off?" Jin asked having a terrible feeling rising in his gut. "Wait you don't have to get serious…yet…?"

The young man removed his blindfold.

Red eyes stared at Jin.

"Oh, damn…"

"Tohari!"

Jin and the white haired assassin looked to find Black Rose running towards them at a fast rate. Jin was relieved.

"Tohari, you take the other one! I'll handle him!"

Jin nodded and escaped, while the white haired assassin was distracted. In a second's time Lani burst out of nowhere and landed in front of Jin. Her eyes however, were fixed on Black Rose.

"How dare you run away from me! I'll get you for this!" Lani seethed.

Jin held out his arm.

"No, I'm your opponent."

Lani turned a sour look towards Jin, but then it brightened.

"You're kinda cute," Lani said materializing a sword. "Lil' Miss Prophecy has good taste."

Jin smirked.

"Doesn't she?"

Lani charged and Jin followed. Their weapons clashed. Jin could feel the excitement run through his body as he avoided and countered Lani's attacks. Jin ducked under Lani's blade and thrust his body upward. Lani looked surprised and jumped backwards just in time to save herself injury. Jin saw a couple of strands of hair fly off her head and he smirked. Lani glared at Jin, after she checked to see if anything else was close to falling out.

"You're gonna pay for that, boy!" Lani growled. "Do you know how long it took for me to get it this way?"
Jin smirked.

"It wasn't very nice to begin with," he replied smugly.

Without warning, Lani charged at Jin and threw her weapon at him. With a startled cry Jin ducked out of the way, but another weapon was coming to where he was falling. In a reflex Jin twisted his body so that he dodged the weapon and safely made it to the ground. His heart was beating quickly, but the thrill made him want more.

"You're pretty good," Lani said grinning. "I'm kinda sorry I'm gonna kill ya."
Jin stood up and materialized his weapon again.

"Is there any way that we won't have to kill one another?" Jin asked.
Lani shook her head.

"You're a danger to Bluse and Raifelle. If ya die, then we don't have to worry about there bein' trouble," Lani replied.

"But why are you trying to kill the host?" Jin asked. "What can he possibly do?"
Lani smirked.

"Kill the host, kill the monster," Lani replied. "Ya know too much anyway."

Jin did not get to ask any more questions because Lani charged once more. They fought mercilessly for minutes. Jin felt a tingle and in the corner of his eye saw Black Rose disappear after the white haired assassin. He heard clashes in the air and saw flashes of light that told him Black Rose and the white haired young man were fighting hard.

Just then Lani took Jin by surprised and attacked him. A searing pain cut through his arm and he staggered backwards. Blood gushed out of his arm and Jin winced. He had no idea her sword was so sharp. *Of course its sharp stupid,* Jin thought in poor humor.

Jin glared at Lani, who came running at him again. Jin ran forward and their weapons collided again. Something solid inside of Jin chipped off and he felt his body take control.

Jin lunged at Lani; engaging her in battle with everything he had. He had to work hard in order for the prophecy to be fulfilled. He wanted Cayn to be happy, no matter what happened to him. Jin thrust his weapon into Lani and she was sent crashing into the ground. He jumped after her with his sword raised and it caught in the ground. Jin growled and looked up to Lani, jumping on the roof. Jin followed quickly.

"You're not getting away!" Jin cried as he transported in front of Lani. Lani looked surprised and jumped back, but not in time to escape the damage. Jin slashed into her leg.

"Ya don't give a girl a break, do ya?" Lani said staggering back. Jin noticed how her leg trembled.

"You were planning on killing me this whole time," Jin said incredulously. "How do you expect me to give you a break?"

Lani smirked.

"I don't."

"Behind you!!" Black Rose's voice cried.

Everything suddenly slowed down around Jin. Lani was charging forward, with her weapon aimed at his heart. He was turning around. The white haired assassin was behind him with his weapon coming down on him and Black Rose was running towards him, with a panicked expression on her face.

Jin was shoved to the ground.

A bloodcurdling scream pierced his ears.

Crimson liquid spattered on Jin's body.

Everything sped back to normal pace. Black Rose crumpled onto the floor of the roof- lifeless. Her mask floated into the puddle of crimson. Jin's eyes widened. With shaky hands he touched his face and felt the wetness. He looked at his hands and they were covered in her blood. Jin was not sure if he screamed or not.

"He looks kinda scared," Lani said with a grin. Her body was covered in blood.

"She should not have been watching you," the white haired young man said. He gave a small nudge to Xia's motionless body. Something else chipped off inside of Jin and then it cracked. Jin lunged over Xia's body. His eyes flashed red. The white haired man and Lani stepped back, unnerved.

"Don't touch her!" Jin snarled. He clutched Xia's body and turned her over.

"Wake up!" he cried. "Why the hell are you dead at a time like this?!"

"I am not dead… you idiot. So stop screaming in my ear."

Jin's eyes widened and Xia's opened slightly Jin hushed her and placed a hand to her cheek. It was almost bloodless.

"You ain't dead yet?" Lani asked surprised.

"I certainly thought we had you for sure," the white haired man said scoffing.

Jin's hands were shaking. Xia could feel him tightening his grip on her body. Something hard inside of Jin cracked and crumbled into pieces. Xia gasped.

"Calm down Tohari!" she muttered quickly. Xia's breath caught and she coughed, setting her aching lungs on fire. Jin's shaking did not cease and it frightened her. Jin's eyes were red.

"Do not talk *hanev*," Jin's voice was deeper and darker than usual. "Reserve your energy."

Xia tried to speak again but she coughed again and writhed in pain. Jin took off his school jacket and placed it under Xia's head.

"Jin… please…" Xia's voice was feeble.

Jin grinned a slow smile.

"Close your eyes *hanev*," Jin's red eyes glowed and his hair began to grow and change color. "Close your eyes *hanev*. I do not want you to witness this."

Xia had tears running down her cheeks. She was in so much pain but she did not care.

"Not right now Jin," Xia pleaded, "… please come back."

Jin's thumb ran across Xia's bottom lip tenderly. Xia stared back at him with wide and frightened eyes. Jin gently lifted Xia's head and gazed at her. His honey colored eyes were filled with warmth. Jin closed his eyes and lowered his head until his lips met Xia's. Her eyes grew wide. Jin pulled away with opened eyes.

"Sorry, Xia," he said before smiling. "But I didn't want you to expect it."

Xia found his smile to be almost… happy.

"Jin…"

Jin shut his eyes again and a bright light engulfed everyone. Xia felt her body tingle and warmth filled her. Her body felt as if the blood inside of her was working more than usual. The light that came from Jin's body somehow healed her.

The light slowly disappeared and with it Jin's body. In its place was a young man with long, crimson colored hair that pooled onto the rooftop and blood-red eyes. On his back were large brilliant white wings. A tinkle, the sound of a small bell rang through the night. The winds picked up, the trees whistled and the chiming of the bell became fiercer. On one of his wings was a ring made of bright gold. His arms held the descriptions Jin's had, but his seemed to move in the moonlight.

"Jin is no longer here…*hanev*."

"Cayn…"

Tears came out of Xia's eyes and Cayn wiped them away tenderly. The shining around his body stopped, and his marking s seemed to dull as well.

"Close your eyes now, *hanev* and do not open them until I am done."

Xia closed her eyes and did not open them again. She heard the screams of Lani and heard her bones crush. Xia cringed. Something akin to a growl escaped the other assain.

Words Xia could not understand were exchanged between Cayn and the white haired assassin before Xia heard the sounds of weapons clashing. She counted three seconds and then the other assassin let out a cry of pain. How powerful was this man? Xia's heart beat out of fear.

A few more words were said and Cayn's voice had a hint of coolness to his anger. Xia opnend her eyes against her better judgement and watched Cayn take a step toward the white haired assassin. For a second nothing moved but then in a flash, Cayn held his hand through the assassin's throat. His nails were long and sharp, like unsheathed swords. The white haired assassin opened his mouth but no scream was heard. Blood dripped down Cayn's extended nails, making a river flow down his hands.

Xia watched the blood fall in droplets onto the rooftop. A small pool of blood was forming at Cayn's feet.

Plip

Plip

Plip

Cayn removed his hand from the man's throat. The white haired assassin fell to the ground. Cayn's lips curled into a sickening grin.

Cayn slowly turned to Xia. His lips were still smiling.

His eyes glowed with the gleam of the moon, in the darkness of the night.

Xia let out the scream that had been threatening to escape since she first opened her eyes. She felt her mind go blank and body go numb. Everything shut down and Xia fell unconscious with wide, frightened and tear filled eyes.

*   *   *

"Thank-you for coming on such short notice Cayn-*kai*," Neisei said kissing the cheeks of the red haired young man in front of him. Intense crimson eyes looked up into his brown ones and Neisei took a step back. The young man sighed and pushed his long curtain-red ponytail behind his shoulder.

"Do my eyes unsettle you as well?" Cayn asked in a quiet voice.

Neisei nodded.

"They do," he started, "because they hold a disquiet in them."

Cayn closed his eyes and turned away from Neisei.

"Was it wrong of me to show myself so early on?" he asked in a still, quiet tone of voice. His eyes followed an invisible downcast line, eyelids half closed.

"...She is unfamiliar with you, Cayn-*kai*. I think it was still too early for her to see *that* you," Neisei replied.

Cayn closed his eyes and opened them again. He turned to face Neisei but kept his gaze on the floor.

"And with you?" he questioned. "Are my eyes frightening?"

"Be rest assured, I am the only one here who is still unsettled. My wife is very fond of them," Neisei explained. "Please, let me show you to her."

Neisei smiled and led Cayn into the sitting room. Tudios had tea prepared and was setting in front of Toi and Are. She smiled when she noticed Cayn.

"My, how you have grown," she said smiling and kissing both his cheeks. "I remember you when you were just a boy a little older than Aya."

A smirk faintly played on Cayn's lips.

"It has been a while, Tudios-*pi*," Cayn said softly.

Are giggled.

"*Kanti*! Come sit by your *kohnah*!" Are said grinning. "I haven't actually had time to give you a look yet."

155

Cayn nodded and moved to sit by his mother respectfully. However, his face held a little skepticism.

"What *kohnah* is saying is that you have not been out of your room for two days and she is worried," Toi said smiling. Cayn turned his head towards Toi and smiled warmly.

"*Kohvah*," Cayn whispered.

"*Kanti*," Toi said gently.

"I am glad you are getting along with your parents Cayn-*kai*," Neisei said smiling.

Cayn nodded. Are and Toi shared a smile. A short silence entered the room. Cayn sat still while he sipped his tea. The smell and taste were comforting to him, but the situation was far more overwhelming. He promised himself not to eat until she did. Her look haunted him, those pretty tear-filled eyes. Did his woman even realize the pain she was causing him? Cayn grinned grimly. He could bet anything that she did not even care how much she hurt him.

"I wanted to ask you all for your assistance," Tudios said breaking the silence. "As you know, *quelpi* will not leave her room."

Cayn felt his heart ache and rubbed it.

"We have asked her a number of times to tell us what the problem is, but she does not reply to us," Neisei explained softly. Pain was laced in his attractive voice.

"It has been three days and we did not want to rush her, but she will not eat a thing. Surely this is not healthy for a young girl such as herself?"

Toi gently placed his teacup back onto its saucer.

"Has she said anything at all?" he asked. "Anything that we can use to help her get better?"

"And has she really not eaten anything?" Are questioned.

Tudios looked at her husband, who gave her a small nod.

"When she is in her right mind she has said that she wants Jin-*kai* back," Tudios replied. "And Neisei's concen needs to be corrected. She eats very little."

"What do you mean by 'in her right mind?'" Are asked concerned.

Tudios and Neisei share a worried look.

"...She has nightmares and screams until her throat is raw," Neisei replied. "When she is like this, we cannot enter the room."

"It's as if she is frightened by us," Tudios continued with tears in her eyes.

"That is my fault. She rejects me as she is supposed to," Cayn said quietly. The words she said before she fell unconscious repeated in Cayn's head. "*You monster! Filthy creature!*" Did she even know she said them?

They hurt so much that rubbing his heart only made it worse. Only his *hanev* could be able to understand him the way he needed her to.

But what would she dream if she knew how he felt when he killed those people?

"She is not supposed to!" Are snapped. "It is our fault for having the two of them become so attached and then rip them apart. But we knew this had to happen. Still..."

"It hurts," Toi finished for his wife. He rubbed her back in a comforting way. Cayn looked away from his parents. A bitter feeling was starting to make its way up his body and settle in his heart- making it heavier than it was before.

"Tell me, Cayn-*kai* does this hurt Jin as well?" Neisei asked noticing the pained look that crossed Cayn's features. Cayn shook his head.

"No. He purposely is not showing again until she learns to accept it all," Cayn replied. "This will not be painful for him ever again."

Hanev

Cayn slowly sat down outside the door to Xia's room. It had been two weeks since she had last spoken to him. Cayn knew that she was angry that Jin was gone and Cayn was the right person to take her anger out on. But she did not know how much he missed her voice… and Cayn could not tell her. He was her *hanev* and she was his. Being away from something he wanted so badly, made his heart ache. It was more painful than he would have ever imagined it to be.

Cayn gently pushed his long ponytail over his shoulder and rested his head against the door. She actually agreed to speak with him; even though it was through the door. It was better than nothing and Cayn wanted nothing more than to hear her voice again. Cayn closed his eyes and waited for her to talk.

"…Are you there?" Xia's voice said. It sounded well enough, considering she was still miserable. Cayn nodded.

"I am," he said.

"Are my parents there as well?" Xia's voice asked.

"I asked them to leave us be," Cayn replied.

Neither of them said anything for a while.

"…Are you angry with me?"

Cayn's lips formed a small smirk.

"No," he replied shortly.

"Even though I was angry with you?" Xia asked meekly.

Cayn's lips opened a little more and a sigh escaped.

"Yes."

"Even *though* I was angry with you?" Xia asked again with a little more force.

Cayn nodded again.

"*Yes,*" Cayn replied with as much force as Xia used.

Xia did not reply for a minute and Cayn relished in the silence.

"Tell me then," her voice started, "why are you still trying to speak with me? You cannot think that I will leave this room."

"I try to speak with you because I love your voice," Cayn said. "I am *hanev* so I can tell you this. I do not shame telling you this, but only you."

"…Are we *bavdnah* because of the prophecy?" Xia's voice asked with a hint of bitterness in it.

Cayn shook his head knowing Xia could not see it.

"I am *hanev* by choice," Cayn replied softly.

"How can you be *hanev* by choice? There is no way that can happen for us!" Xia said tearfully.

Cayn wanted to wipe her sadness away, but it was not going to leave her if he simply took his fingers and caressed her.

"Then why do you bother to fight it?" Cayn asked.

Xia was silent.

"I have known you for the longest of times, *hanev*," Cayn said smiling faintly. "I have known of you long before I knew Jin."

Xia did not say anything. Cayn closed his eyes and listened to Xia sniff and wipe away her tears.

"*Hanev?*" Cayn asked softly.

"…Yes?" Xia replied.

Cayn lifted his hands to the door as if feeling Xia at his fingertips.

"How long to you plan on being upset with me?" Cayn asked.

Xia did not reply for minutes. Cayn smiled softly. She was thinking about it.

"For as long as it takes for me to hit you," she snapped.

Cayn nodded.

"You may do whatever you please then, *hanev*," Cayn said. "If it will make you happy, then you may hit me as hard as you see fit."

159

Xia let out a watery laugh and Cayn felt relieved.

"...I have been stupid," Xia said softly.

Cayn opened his eyes and stared at the ceiling.

"Undoubtedly," Cayn said.

"Can you forgive me?" Xia's voice asked.

Cayn smirked.

"Let me propose a deal."

Xia was silent for a moment.

"What type of deal?" she finally questioned, voice cautious.

"You will see when you come out to hit me."

Xia did not say anything else for a while. Cayn felt a bit of laughter escape his throat.

"...If that is what it takes," Xia finally muttered.

Cayn nodded. She had to see it his way. He had suffered enough.

"*Hanev?*" Cayn asked.

"Yes?"

"Are you hungry?"

"I am."

"I am going to bring you something to eat."

"As long as you keep the door closed and walk away."

Cayn nodded and stood up.

"I will return shortly," Cayn said in his deep voice.

"Okay."

Cayn felt relieved and walked away from Xia's door. It took a few weeks, but they could finally move on. Cayn walked down the stairs to find his parents and Xia's parent's looking at him worriedly.

"Did she say anything to you?" Tudios asked as soon as Cayn reached the bottom step.

"She has told me that she is ready to forgive me and that she is hungry," Cayn replied.

Are lifted an eyebrow in question.

"Are you alright? You seem to be feeling better," she said.

160

Cayn nodded.

"I am feeling… well," Cayn replied to his mother.

"Did she say anything else to you? Was she still crying?" Neisei asked.

Cayn slowly turned to Neisei with a small curve to his lips.

"Yes and yes."

He smiled warmly and walked in the direction of the kitchen.

"Tudios-*pi,* would you mind if I used your kitchen for a moment?" Cayn asked. "*Hanev* is hungry and I will not keep her waiting any longer."

"Use anything you would like…" Tudios said faintly.
Cayn nodded and exited into the kitchen.

"You have a strong willed young man," Neisei said grinning. "I am so glad he has opened Xia…"
Tudios nodded.

"I was beginning to worry that he would not be able to," Tudios said quietly.

"He has," Toi said with his arm around his wife's shoulder, "that's what counts."

Are looked after Cayn with a soft expression on her face.

"Cayn loves her so much," Are said. "I don't think he would allow failure."

Another week passed and Cayn was officially impatient. Xia would continue to tell him that he had to wait in order to see her. She insisted that she was not ready to see him yet and he had to be patient. Cayn walked up the stairs to Xia's room with his patience at an end. He noticed that her door was open, which surprised him. Cayn took a step forward to peer into her room.

"Stop where you are."
Cayn stopped all movement, with a smirk on his face.

"*Hanev,*" Cayn said in his deep voice. "You are out of your room."

"Yes I am," Xia said. "I just wanted to get a look at you before you saw me."

Cayn chuckled.

"Now that you have, may I turn around?" he asked.

"I still have to hit you," Xia said.

"And I still get to hold you until I forgive you," Cayn said.

Xia did not say anything for a second.

"You can turn if you want," she said.

Cayn smirked and turned around to Xia's slap. Cayn held his cheek for a moment and closed his eyes. After seconds, he opened them again and looked at Xia. An almost menacing grin spread across his lips. Xia's eyes widened.

"Why are you looking at me like that?" Xia asked in a slightly frightened voice.

Cayn held his grin.

"Are you satisfied?" Cayn replied. "Now I have to forgive you."

Xia looked as if she were not very keen on the idea. Cayn walked over to Xia and touched his finger to her cheek. The expression on his face was unreadable.

"You have the most amazing texture to your skin," Cayn said softly. "It's so soft and smooth, like a newborn."

Xia flushed, but a cautious and confused expression was on her face. Cayn gently ran his finger over Xia's cheek, to her jaw and slid his fingers to her chin. His thumb tenderly stroked Xia's bottom lip. The whole time he did not speak.

"Cayn..." Xia said with a mixture of vexation and embarrassment.

"This is part of my proposition. Do not interrupt me," Cayn replied.

Xia's eye twitched in annoyance.

"How dare you...!" she started to growl, but Cayn tilted her head upwards slightly. Xia's eyes grew wide.

"What in the world are you doing?!" Xia cried trying to pull away. Cayn leaned even closer to Xia until they were less than an inch away from each other.

Xia wanted to say something, but a mixture of fear and panic was starting to settle in. For a moment nothing moved. Cayn was inhaling Xia's scent, commiting it to memory.

Something came out of her throat that sounded like a protest. At once, Cayn pressed his lips firmly to Xia's in a tender kiss. Xia froze and after a second, Cayn released her lips.

"You say too much with your words, *hanev,*" Cayn replied.

Xia was angry but could not help blushing. She also took note of how quickly her heart was beating. Who was this man to just *come on* to her like that?

"I have forgiven you," Cayn said pulling away.

"That quickly?" Xia asked bitterly.

Cayn nodded with a sly smirk playing on his lips.

"Do not think I do not hear the dissatisfaction in your tone, *hanev,*" Cayn started, "because you agreed to this proposition of mine."

Xia nodded reluctantly.

"I will do my best not to be *dissatisfied* in front of you," she snapped angrily. "Who do you think you are, you monster?"

Cayn took hold of Xia's hand. His lips were firmly placed in a wily smirk.

"Do whatever you see fit, *hanev* but I assure you, I will break you out of all your foul moods and show you the monster I really am."

Xia actually felt a grin come to her face. She was glad it was there because to a degree, Cayn scared her. But right now Cayn was challenging her... and it felt good.

"Then I assure you, Cayn-*kai* that I will live up to your challenge," Xia said strongly enough, but something inside of her knew it would be a short matter of time before her resolve broke down.

"Do you really mean this?" he asked unable to keep the excitement from his low voice. Cayn wanted the two of them to be real *hanev* and fulfill the prophecy. But he first needed her to come out of the hole she had dug herself into. She was *hanev* first and foremost. *His hanev.*

Ever since he was little he knew a little girl in Bluse would be his *hanev*. He just needed to find her. Finally, she was standing before him telling him that she would try to be *hanev* or rather; she would fight him until she approved of herself highly enough for the title of *hanev*. Still, the ache inside of Cayn slowly ebbed away.

"Yes," Xia replied. "But tell me the truth about this. Is Jin really gone?"

Cayn smiled and shook his head but his crimson eyes were sharp.

"No," he replied. "He will not disappear. He will just remain inside of me."

Xia nodded, looking away.

"Why didn't you tell me before?" she asked.

Cayn held Xia's hand over his heart.

"Because *we* are *hanev*," he replied simply.

"But did Jin agree to this too?" Xia asked. "Why?"

Cayn gently squeezed Xia's hand.

"Would you have loved me because I am your *hanev*?" Cayn asked.

Xia held her head high and looked into Cayn's crimson eyes.

"I really don't know," she replied.

Cayn nodded.

"I want you to find the answer in me," Cayn said softly. He let go of Xia's hand.

Xia was blushing and glared.

"How can you say these things so easily?" Xia asked.

"I am *hanev*," Cayn replied. He gently caressed Xia's cheek before leading her down the stairs to their parents.

*　　*　　*

Xia was loosing the challenge terribly.

Xia's face was red and there was nothing she could do to stop it. Everything about her *bavdnah* made her want to really believe that they could be together as he wanted it to be, but at the same time, he made her upset by just being next to her. He had a way of influencing her to think things that she thought only Jin could and doing it by saying no more than ten words at a time.

That made Xia even more confused and embarrassed.

But at the same time, it made her strangely attracted to him.

Xia found it very easy to be attracted to Cayn simply because he was a very beautiful person. Cayn had a very handsome face. It was young, but so exotic and new to her. His eyes were not as threatening as she first thought they were. They held so much warmth and love in them that it made Xia unsure of what to do around him. His expression was so serious, but every time he told her she was something important to him, his face would change and his melting stare would make her mad.

After spending another few weeks with him, Xia found out that he did not speak nearly as much as she would have like him to. She had grown very fond of his deep voice. Somehow, it managed to stir even the deepest part of Xia and make her listen to whatever he had to say. Cayn closed his eyes sometimes and Xia would take the opportunity to scrutinize every detail of his perfect face. When she did, a feeling would well up inside of her and she would battle the urge to touch him. Xia's finger's longed to trace the features of Cayn's lovely face. His perfect red brows, high cheekbones, straight nose, full lips. Xia was fighting to find something wrong with her *bavdnah,* but every time pinpointed some fault, another good thing would fill its place.

Xia found him very frustrating.

"Why don't I feel as if I'm betraying Jin?" Xia questioned her reflection in the mirror. "Curse that no good, stuck-up little pretty boy!"

Xia closed her eyes and wished she knew what she was feeling, and became confused all over again. She had just finished that stage with Jin and now moved onto Cayn in a matter of weeks. She could not help it. Cayn was just something she could not avoid and get over. He was hers since the day he was born and she was his since she was born. They were destined to be together and as much as she thought she did not want him, the truth was, she wanted him very much.

"*Hanev...* may I come in?" Cayn's voice said quietly.

Xia jumped and looked around her room, making sure everything was in order.

"Come in!" Xia said diving onto her bed.

Cayn stood in Xia's doorway, looking better with every look. He had a perfect fitting black three-quarter length shirt on with a white shirt under it. His pants were crisp and white and Xia noticed a small chain sticking out of the back pocket. His long red hair was tied in a ponytail on his head. He had little strands of hair sticking out over his forehead. Xia thought they added to his looks- if anything else could possibly be added. Cayn had a very nice complexion according to Xia because he was not as pale as she was. *He looks like a normal teenager from Hainai,* Xia thought as she looked Cayn over. *With the exception of the red hair and eyes...and wings that are tucked away...*

In his hand was a long box wrapped in pretty navy blue paper. It was finished in a small white bow. Xia looked at it interested. She was not used to gifts. Cayn smiled, which sent Xia's heart fluttering. He walked into the room and closed the door behind him. Xia sat up and smiled. Did Cayn have any idea how hard her heart was beating?

"How are you today?" Cayn asked and sat down at her desk.

Xia shrugged.

"I'm fine," Xia replied. "How are you?"

Cayn's lips curled delicately.

"Magnificent."

Xia's face burned. *Why did he smile like that? Why did he respond like that? Why does he look like that?* Xia thought flushed. She cursed his ever attractive voice. Cayn handed Xia the box and she took it.

"May I open it now?" Xia asked.

"Surely I thought you did not want any gifts from someone like me," Cayn said. Xia's eye twitched in annoyance. He was smirking that sly, all-knowing *annoying* grin. Xia flipped her hair behind her shoulders and made a point of pulling off the ribbon in front of Cayn's face. Amusement twinkled in his eyes.

Xia took hold of the paper and pulled. She noticed that the wrapping was covered in blue lace. Xia's eye lit up in interest as she fingered the paper. Before she made the first rip, Xia glanced at Cayn who was looking at her amusedly. Xia gave him a smile before turning her attention back to the package. She ripped away the navy blue wrapping paper and in her hand was a long velvet box.

"Is this for me?" Xia asked incredulous. She looked at Cayn suspiciously, wanting to know exactly what the crimson-eyed young man was planning.

Cayn nodded. Xia fingered the long box unsure if she wanted to open it. Suddenly, Cayn's fingers enveloped her hand and slowly cracked the box open. Inside the box was a thin gold box-chain with a small black rose attached to it. Xia's eyes grew wide as she touched the gift.

"It's beautiful!"

Cayn smiled. He took the chain out of the box and held it in his fingers.

"Turn around."

Xia quickly turned so her back was facing Cayn. She felt his fingers gently move her hair over her shoulder, then fasten the chain around her neck. Xia touched the necklace and turned back around. She smiled and threw her arms around Cayn.

"It's beautiful! Thank-you!"

Cayn closed his eyes and rested his head on Xia's shoulder.

"You are welcome, *hanev,*" he said. His voice made Xia lightheaded. It sounded better every time he opened his mouth.

"Isn't this the cutest thing?"

Xia looked and Cayn turned around to see Are and Tudios in the doorway and their husbands behind them.

"Are-*pi, mothi!*" Xia said surprised. She and Cayn broke apart. Xia coughed to the side looking away.

"*Kanti* your father and I would love to talk to you," Are said in a singsong voice.

"I will make sure this moment never leaves my heart, dearest," Cayn said smirking. Xia glared at him, but her cheeks were burning.

Cayn gently stroked Xia's hand before leaving her room. The Tohari family went into the sitting room and Xia was left with her parents. Something felt suspicious to her.

"My *quelpi* what a beautiful necklace you are wearing," Neisei said walking into the room. He fingered the necklace lightly.

"Yes," Xia said, "...Cayn-*pi* bought it for me."

Xia heard voice coming from downstairs but she couldn't understand what they were saying.

"Is it still 'Cayn-*pi*'?" Tudios asked. She sighed, "I was hoping for *bavdnah* by now."

"*Mothi!*" Xia said flushing. She was still in the middle of trying to dislike the red haired annoyance.

"I think... your mother is correct," Neisei said smiling. He sat by his daughter and took her hand.

"Have you not yet forgiven him?" Neisei asked.
Xia hung her head low.

"I have *fadi* but..."

"What do you have against calling him *bavdnah*?" Neisei questioned.

Xia shrugged.

"I don't know," she replied, "it just feels embarrassing to me…"

Tudios tittered and Xia looked up.

"I remember you telling Jin-*kai* that *bavdnah* is more than just a lover, *quelpi*," Tudios said with amusement in her voice. "Could it be that you do not fully understand its meaning?"

Xia looked confused.

"What do you mean?" she asked.

Neisei chuckled.

"To call him *bavdnah* is to give him the highest honor and hold him in the greatest esteem," he explained. "When I call your mother *bavdnah* it comes from everything I have and although I may say it playfully from time to time, there is no other word I can give her that explains to everyone else what she is to me and what I am to her."

"You see Xia, *bavdnah* is very important to us," Tudios started, "but *hanev* to the Andez is an even greater honor."

Xia nodded but she was still confused.

"What does it mean then?" Xia inquired.

Her father and mother smiled at her.

"You will have to ask Cayn-*kai* on your own," Neisei said.

Xia nodded.

"…So it would make you happy if I… tried calling him *bavdnah*?" Xia clarified.

"Very much so," Tudios said smiling.

Xia had a million thoughts running through her head, but only a few stuck. She wanted to make her parents happy and… make Cayn happy. She also wanted to know what *hanev* really meant and why Cayn could call her it with such conviction. Xia grasped the flower around her neck.

She wanted to grow up. Even though her attitude towards Cayn leaned more toward nonchalance, she enjoyed being with him more than she let on. Although, Xia had the distinct feeling Cayn knew exactly how she felt even before she knew how she did.

"I will to my best."

Whispered Fear

Xia stood in the gymnasium of her school, closing her eyes. The whole day dragged because she had no competition. She had nothing to entertain her. Whatever the teachers taught, Xia knew and it had no importance to her life. She was not going to remain in Hainai and work like every other student. She was not going to waste her life being afraid of what was beyond the wall. She was different to the people in Hainai District. She knew that from the start.

A wind blew through the open doors of the gym and Xia walked outside. The sun was bright and warm. It reflected off of the chain Xia never took off her neck.

It was officially break for the Hainai High. Only the students doing sports were in school for practice. All the other students were out having fun, but dreading the return of the school year when vacation was over. Xia would not be coming back here when it was over. She did not want to stay any longer. The false pretenses of her 'training' were over and it was finally time to retaliate. Bluse had tricked her for too long.

Xia exited the schoolyard and looked back for a second.

"Farewell," she said before walking out the gate.

Xia was going to leave Hainai District altogether to learn about the Andez. She wanted to know everything there was to know about Cayn and his parents. She wanted to know their culture so that she could learn how to make him happy because Cayn made her happier that she thought she would ever be. Xia and Cayn were going to leave in the evening because it would be easier to leave without causing trouble.

Cayn Tohari was waiting for her by the gate looking better as time went on. He wore dark sunshades, a white dress shirt and khakis. His hair was tied in his customary ponytail at the top of his head and his wings were tucked away so his appearance would be normal. Xia grinned. They were going to Andez because it was the only place that did not fear the prophecy coming true.

"Have you finished?" he asked.

Xia nodded.

"Did Jin want to say goodbye?" Xia asked.

Cayn shook his head.

"Jin has already finished," Cayn replied.

Xia nodded and began walking down the street into town. Her mother and Are wanted to buy more clothes for the journey to Andez. Xia did not mind but she was a little embarrassed with Cayn around. She wanted him to be there, but she was afraid her heart would give in. Xia and Cayn made their way to the store her mom and Are were in. Cayn held the door for her and she blushed while walking in.

"Xia! Cayn!" Are said excitedly. "Over here!"

The words usually spoken could not be said in the street. It would cause too much of a panic. Xia and Cayn walked towards their parents and saw piles of clothes waiting for them.

"You have to try these on Xia!" Tudios said smiling. She had a pile of clothes in her arms.

Xia never saw her mother look so childish before, but she eyed the clothes with weariness. The colors made her dizzy.

"...All of them?" Xia asked.

"They complement your skin tone."

Xia looked up from the pile and saw one of Jin's friends in the store uniform.

"Do they?" Xia asked unsure.

"Yes they do," Erick Bastion said smiling. "I hear you are moving away. Good luck in your new school."

Xia smiled and nodded.

"Thank-you," she said, hauling the clothes into a changing room.

"Erick…" Cayn said softly.

Erick turned his head in Cayn's direction and smiled.

"Have we met before?" Erick asked politely.

Cayn shook his head.

"Excuse me, I mistook you for someone else," Cayn said quickly.

Erick shrugged.

"You got my name right, so don't worry. You...remind me of my friend Jin, but I don't know why. You look nothing alike," Erick said in an offhand manner.

Cayn nodded with a smirk on his lips.

"He moved away a few weeks ago," Erick continued. "Mrs. Chang, did you know Jin was convinced that Xia was Black Rose? Come to think of it I haven't seen her in a while either. Maybe they went off together."

Erick and Are snickered.

"Yes, Xia had told me that," Tudios said tittering. "But I do not see how that is possible."

"Is Jin happy where he is now Mrs. Tohari?" Erick questioned Are.

Are nodded.

"Very happy," she replied, "and amused. Oh, I almost forgot Erick. I think the reason Cayn reminds you of Jin is because they are brothers."

Erick turned to Cayn with a surprised expression on his face.

"Well then it's nice to meet you," Erick said holding out his hand. "I'm Erick Bastion. I was Jin's best friend."

Cayn shook Erick's hand.

"Cayn Tohari. Jin's older brother," Cayn said.

Xia walked out of the dressing room holding the pile.

"They all fit," she said. "Thank-you Erick. They look very nice."

"It is my pleasure to help you," Erick said. "Can I help you with anything else?"

Tudios and Are nodded and started talking about clothes for Cayn. Xia placed the pile of clothes back onto the chair and watched her mother and Cayn's mother walk around the store to sort things out. Cayn sat beside her.

"Our parents are very energetic aren't they?" Xia asked.

Cayn nodded.

"Very," he replied. But his eyes were following Erick.

*　　*　　*

Xia finished packing the last of her belongings and looked around her room. She was finally leaving Hainai District to return to the outside world. She was ready. Xia walked over to the windowsill and picked up the dead rose she had failed to throw away. It had been such a pretty flower once and the fact that Jin gave it to her, made it all the more pretty. Pink turning red. Xia smiled and took the flower out of the vase. She opened her window and dropped the flower out of it.

"You were right Jin," she said as she watched the wind blow the dead petals across the walkway. "But because of that I can move on."

Xia smiled and turned around walking back to her suitcase.

"It's kind of hard to hate someone who loves you so much," she said to herself and laughed. "Again you were right Jin. He's grown on me."

Xia carried the bags out of her room down the stairs, just as Cayn was walking up them. He looked almost surprised.

"*Hanev* let me carry those for you!" he said and took the bags from Xia. She learned that it was pointless to refute him. He would either ignore her or give her a smoldering look that made her shut right up.

"Thank-you," Xia said smiling. She realized that she smiled more than ever when she was around Cayn.

"Do not thank me for such menial labor," Cayn said walking down the stairs.

Xia huffed but grinned.

"Fine then. I won't," she said flinging her hair behind her shoulders.

Xia could tell Cayn was smirking.

"Good," he said. Xia loved everything about her life right now. Even though her people would not accept her, even though she had made no friends in Hainai, even though Jin was gone, Xia never felt happier.

"*Quelpi* are you ready?" Neisei asked as his daughter walked down the stairs. "You will not be coming back here for a while."

Xia nodded and smiled. Aya Tohari peeked from behind Tudios and ran into her brother with a huge smile on her face.

"Cayn is going away too?" Aya asked while Cayn picked her up. She pouted.

"Not at all," Cayn said softly. "You will be coming too but in a few weeks."

"Okies…"

"Good girl. When you get there, I will teach you how to fly," Cayn said kissing his little sister on her cheeks.

"Like you?" Aya asked with wide eyes.

"Only if you are really good to the Chang family," Cayn replied.

Aya hugged Cayn as best she could and squealed in delight.

"I will! I will!" she cried. "And I get to see Jin too!"

Cayn placed his sister back on the floor.

"…I love you. Now be a good girl," he said.

Aya nodded and said her goodbyes to her brother and Xia before heading into the living room. Cayn turned his head to listen to Xia's conversation.

"Do you know why you are doing this *quelpi*?" Tudios asked.

"I want to do this because it will make everyone happy," Xia replied. "But it will make me even happier."

Neisei nodded and smiled warmly. Xia knew he was proud of her, everyone was. Tudios walked over to Xia and gave her a tight hug. Xia wrapped her arms around her mother enjoying the feel of the embrace.

"Be good to Are-*pi* and Toi-*pi*," Tudios said. "And Cayn-*pi* as well."

Xia nodded.

"And eat well, please," Neisei said. "Do write to us about the things you have learned."

Xia nodded again and hugged her father.

"I will," she said. "I have to go now. Are-*ken* and Toi-*kai* are waiting for us at the wall."

Neisei and Tudios nodded. Neisei rested his hand on Cayn's shoulder.

"She is in your hands now," Neisei said.

Cayn nodded.

"I will do my best to protect her," Cayn said.

Neisei nodded.

"Indeed you will."

Cayn smiled and opened the door.

"You will be there for the ceremony?" Cayn asked.

Neisei and Tudios nodded.

"We could not possibly miss it," Tudios said.

Cayn nodded.

"What ceremony?" Xia asked as she made her way out the door. The front door closed and Neisei and Tudios looked at each other.

"She is very cute," Tudios said smiling.

Neisei nodded.

"Perhaps," Neisei said wrapping his arms around Tudios' waist, "we should start with another child while Xia is away."

Tudios giggled as her husband kissed her neck.

"That may be a possibility," she laughed, "if you are good."

"I will be on my best behavior," Neisei said grinning into his wife's neck.

* * *

Cayn and Xia finally reached the wall at nightfall. By the time she arrived Xia's heart was beating in excitement and anticipation. She and Cayn barely spoke on the walk there, but it was natural to her. The two of them had shared so many words while she was getting to know him that she had enough to dwell on without them talking at the moment.

She had only spent a few months with him, but she found that he was shy when speaking to her for fear of saying something wrong. When he had told her that, she had to rub it in but then she started to look at Cayn differently. She was so used to him being so in control of everything that it made Xia really think about how hard it was for him to admit to her his fear. Then again, he did not have the slightest problem reminding her that the two of them were *bavdnah* every chance that he had.

After a while, Xia had to admit to him that she had been longing to touch his face, like he had done to her when they first *really* met. She wanted him to understand her if, by some miracle, she slipped. Cayn smiled at her and told her that she would be able to if she had a little more patience. Then he began rubbing in her confession in her face like she did his own.

Xia and Cayn saw Toi waiting for them at the wall.

"Good evening you two," Toi said smiling. "Just place your things in and hop into the kart."

The kart was a hovercraft with seating for four people and a trunk. It had a large metal ring around it to help passengers in and a steering wheel in front of the driver's seat.

"Where is *kohnah*?" Cayn asked.

Toi smiled.

"She is at the transportation site," Toi replied. "We will meet up with her when we leave."

177

"Okay," Xia said. She helped Cayn place her things in the kart then moved to get in. She was surprised when Cayn moved to help her into the seat. She blushed and thanked him. Cayn nodded and sat next to her. Suddenly, Tekeda Tohari's police kart came into view.

"Toi!" Tekeda said getting out of the kart. "Geez, you really know how to move fast."
Toi smiled.

"Of course I do," Toi said smiling at Tekeda. "Please, meet Miss Xia Chang and you have met Cayn."
Xia said her 'how-do-you-dos' and Cayn nodded.

"I haven't seen you since you were a little kid," Tekeda said surprised.
He placed a hand on Cayn's head.

"Uncle," Cayn said.
Tekeda smiled.

"You looked at me like that right after you changed," Tekeda Tohari said. "But you have grown."
Cayn nodded. Tekeda smiled and turned back to Toi.

"So you're leaving for good then?" Tekeda asked.
Toi shrugged.

"Don't sound so excited," Toi said grinning. "I don't know what they are going to end up like so I can't say for sure."
Tekeda nodded.

"Is Aya coming with you?" he inquired.

"The Chang's are going to drop her off in a couple weeks," Toi replied.
Tekeda nodded.

"Well then, good luck," he said.
Toi nodded.

"Tell your wife I said hello," Toi said smiling.
"Of course."
Toi nodded once more and entered the kart. He started it and it vibrated.

"Tell Are hello for me."

Toi nodded and moved the kart towards the gate. It opened and Toi drove the kart through. Xia looked back and smiled as the gate closed. She did not know how long she was going to be gone, but she was not coming back until she learned enough to satisfy her hunger. Xia felt Cayn's arm slip around her shoulders and she leaned into his chest.

"I'm excited," Xia said smiling. "I can't wait to see the place where you were born and lived."

"I know," Cayn said quietly. Xia thought about everything that was about to happen and blushed. Perhaps she would get enough courage to touch Cayn's face. *I couldn't do that*, Xia thought. She felt Cayn touch her chin and she looked up.

"Welcome home," Cayn said.

Xia sat up and looked around her. The sun was shining on the hills and it reflected off the water they were passing by. Trees were spread out along the road below them and provided the kart with splashes of shade. They were in Bluse in a matter of seconds. Xia smiled and looked behind her. Hainai district looked like a glass bubble. She could look in but when the people looked out they saw nothing but barren land. Xia had been waiting to return to Bluse for such a long time. She had almost forgotten Hainai District was in Bluse territory. That was why her people sent her there but... she was no longer wanted here.

"Bluse is not my home," Xia said closing her eyes and letting the winds blow through her hair. "...Andez is."
Cayn chuckled.

"You are right. My mistake, *hanev*," Cayn said grinning. Xia opened her eyes and looked at Cayn.

"Yeah your mistake," she said making Cayn's shoulder her pillow. The position was unbelievably comfortable to her and she started to drift asleep.

Xia was shaken awake by a loud explosion from behind the hovercraft. Xia shot up, looking around wildly before another explosion rocked the hovercraft. Xia flew forward, but was yanked back by Cayn.

"Are you injured, *hanev*?" Cayn asked.

Xia shook her head. Her heart was beating quickly in her chest. She turned her head to look outside around the kart and saw three people flying after them. Xia gasped.

"They're from Bluse!" Xia cried.

Of course they're from Bluse! We're in Bluse! How many times am I going to forget it? Xia thought feeling a little panicked.

"Acquaintances of yours?" Cayn smirked.

"Shut up."

"Sorry to break up your fight, but I would like it very much if you two did something about this," Toi said smiling. He jerked the steering wheel to the side and Xia flew into Cayn again. She glared at the people chasing them.

"Okay you're asking for it!" Xia growled.

She moved to the edge of the kart and jumped off the edge. Cayn was right behind her. Xia was a little surprised with how high they were, but used her magics to float down to the ground. Cayn landed next to her and in a matter of seconds the three people from Bluse were visible. Xia faintly remembered the faces.

"Woah, dudes, she really did betray us," a young man, Fayte, said materializing a sword. He was dressed in a thick, blue robe that Xia recognized as the soldiers uniform of Bluse.

"*Ken* do you even remember who you're up against?" Another man said smiling amicably. He was also dressed in the Bluse uniform but something was strange about him. He looked like...

"Jin?" Xia ventured confused.

James looked amused.

"Never heard of him," James said with his smile still in place. "But *you're* changing the subject."

"First of all, you guys betrayed me! And second, Bluse is something I know like the back of my hand," Xia replied. *Of course I just forgot that we are in Bluse not a minute ago*, Xia thought.

She did not like how James used such a familiar tone of voice with her.

"Fayte, James, she's not nearly as pretty as you said!" Amalia said. She was not wearing a Bluse uniform, but a green and purple sage's robe from Raifelle.

James laughed.

"You're jealous," he said.

"Yeah just because she looks better than you do, doesn't mean you have to hate her, dude," Fayte said.

Xia's eye twitched in annoyance. Who in the world *were* these nutcases? The fair-haired, fifteen-year-old looked up at Cayn. His face was serious. Xia shook her head and looked back at the bickering trio.

"Enough of this! Who are you?" Xia cried angrily.

The three stopped and grinned. Fayte pointed a finger at Xia.

"We are here to give you a warning Xia Chang!" Fayte said. "If you join that *Ikelidek,* Bluse and Raifelle will wage war against you."

Xia was not too shocked to hear the news but she was upset they used that word on Cayn. She placed her hand on Cayn's arm, feeling that he was getting upset.

"Can I help you with anything else?" Xia asked testily.

"Does the dog want to bite us? He's bearing his fangs," James said sneering at Cayn.

Xia smirked.

"Keep talking and I might just let him," Xia said. "What right do you have to judge him?"

"Do hear yourself, *ken?* The *Ikelidek* has ruined your speech!" James said.

Xia's fist shook. She materialized a rod out of her magics.

"If you *dare* say that word in my presence, I will make it the last thing you say," Xia threatened furiously.

"Woah, chill dude, we're not here to fight!" Fayte said quickly. "We just came to tell you that Bluse and Raifelle means business."

"You can tell them, we do as well!" Xia said.

"One more thing, *kilishthi*," Amalia said quickly.

"What?" Xia asked annoyed.

"The Radicals cannot be trusted. They were given that name for a reason," Amalia said. "They thrive on the blood of the innocent and they even kill their own! That *dog* will not hesitate to slay you."

Xia stared at the three in disbelief. A chuckle escaped her throat. Cayn looked down at her mildly surprised.

"Are you finished? I grow tired of your lies," Xia said after she finished laughing. A serious expression was on her face.

"Do you not believe me?" Amalia sneered. "Then why do you not have the dog tell me otherwise?"

Cayn did not say anything.

"Why are you not speaking? Do you find me correct?" Amalia asked Cayn with a grin. "You *enjoyed* killing your own kind did you not?"

Xia felt her anger flow through her veins. She took a step towards the young woman, Amalia.

"What the heck are you talking about, *ken*?" she yelled. "Keep your lies to yourself!"

Fayte and James started laughing. Xia turned furious eyes towards the pair of them.

"*Ken* do you mean you do not know what she is talking about?" James asked.

"Did your *bavdnah* not tell you?" Fayte asked grinning. He shook his finger at Cayn. "Dude, that's so wrong."

Xia was about to say something when she felt Cayn's hand on her shoulder.

"Yes, explain it to her Radical. Tell her how you killed your own kind!" Amalia laughed her annoying high-pitched laugh.

Xia looked up to a grinning Cayn. His eyes were glowing. Something akin to fear slipped down Xia's spine.

"Do you... want to find out how much I found it pleasing?" Cayn asked taking a step forward. The trio visibly cringed.

"So you admit it Radical?" Amalia asked standing tall.

The curl to Cayn's lips sent shivers down Xia's back. It... frightened her. Xia's eyes widened when Cayn disappeared. The next time she saw him, his fingers were wrapped around Amalia's neck and she was struggling to break free.

"...Would you like me to show *hanev* a demonstration?" Cayn asked in low tones.

"Cayn!" Xia cried. "Stop it!"

Cayn chuckled and tightened his grip around his prisoner's neck. Amalia made gurgling noises while she clawed at Cayn's fingers. Long scratches marked Cayn's hands.

"Why are you not answering my question? Is it too difficult for you?" Cayn snarled. His hands were dripping blood.

"*Cayn*! Let her go!" Xia yelled again. She wanted to run to him but her feet were rooted to the ground.

Fayte and James lunged towards Cayn with their weapons raised. He easily avoided them and laughed. Cayn threw Amalia to the ground.

"Did the dog bite you?" Cayn asked laughing. "I am so sorry." His eyes were glowing red.

"Do not provoke us Radical! We are protected under Raifelle!" Fayte said. He was lifting the coughing Amalia off the ground.

"Am I supposed to cower like you?" Cayn asked amused.

"No. But I have your precious *bavdnah*," James called. Cayn slowly turned his head to James who had his arm around Xia's neck. A terrifying expression was on Cayn's face.

"I will assure you, *kai*," Cayn spat, "that if you touch her further; it will cost you your life."

Xia was more frightened than Amalia would ever be. James smirked.

"Then I will leave you with a farewell gift," James said, "...and wait for the day you come for me."

Xia felt dread run through her veins.

She felt James's fingers on her jaw and found herself staring at him with wide eyes. She was trying to get away, but nothing seemed to work. It was not registering fast enough that she was in a bad situation or that no matter how much she tried her blows to his body would seem to go right through him.

"Get...away from me!" Xia cried but was silenced with James's lips. Her body became paralyzed with shock. James pressed firmly into Xia's lips until she felt a sharp pain. Xia suddenly became heavy.

"Until next time *bavda,*" Xia heard James say before she fell unconscious.

*   *   *

"We are here," Toi's words were spoken all too soon. Xia felt herself being shaken awake.

"*Hanev* it is time to wake up," Cayn's soothing voice said in her ear. Xia jumped and held her ear. She glared accusingly at Cayn.

"It is time to wake up, *hanev,*" Cayn said smirking.

"I know that!" Xia said groggily. She looked around confused.

"What... happened?" Xia asked slowly. Then it all hit her. "Wait! Where are those Bluse? A-and the Raifelle? What happened?"

Cayn silenced Xia's ranting by lifting his hand in the air.

"They fled," Cayn replied.

"The cowards!" Xia cried angrily. She wanted to kill the Bluse that kissed her. Xia wiped off her mouth furiously.

"That… coward," she muttered. Tears stung her eyes and Xia found that she was mad at herself.

Cayn was silent. Xia's fist shook in anger. Who were they to jeopardize her mission? Who did that man think he was to just kiss her like that?

With an angry cry, Xia slammed her fist against the side of the kart. Cayn silently watched her, before moving to exit the hovercraft. Xia still had questions for him but let him walk away. Her gaze followed the path his flowing crimson hair cut through the air, as he walked. Her fist was still shaking in anger.

Curse it all! Xia thought angrily. She was not as angry at the trio as she was with herself. Cayn frightened her more than she wanted to admit to herself. Xia slammed her fist against the kart again. A sharp stinging shot through her hand. She ignored the pain. Cayn was not the moster here! How could she just let James kiss her and get away with it?

"Is this how *bavdnah* is supposed to act?" she questioned herself bitterly. Xia moved to slam her fist once more but a hand caught her wrist.

"You will injure yourself if you continue to do this recklessly," Cayn said. His voice sounded rough.

"I don't care," Xia said barely above a whisper. She was still upset with herself, but being next to him did not scare her.

Cayn slid his fingers down Xia's wrist until they were wrapped around her hand. He lifted her pale fingers to his mouth and kissed them tenderly. His eyes were closed leaving his long lashes to brush his cheekbones.

"I am just as that girl said. I enjoyed it," Cayn said in husky tones. His eyelids lifted to reveal glowing crimson orbs. "I will erase all traitors from the face of this earth and I will do it laughingly."

Even after hearing him, the fear would not come back to her. Why did she not want to run from him now?

"That face… Cayn…" Xia breathed.

Cayn smirked.

"What will you do?" he questioned.

"I will protect you from that face inside of you," Xia replied determinedly.

Cayn leaned a little closer to Xia, letting her see his face even more.

"I *am* that face."

Xia glared for a long time into Cayn's handsome features. Cayn smirked and placed one hand on her waist and the other under her hand and helped Xia out of the kart. Xia thanked him, but was unable to look him in the eye. If it was not one thing, it was another and she was still unnerved by that grin.

"Cayn-*pi* isn't she the cutest thing waking up?" Are asked out of nowhere.

Xia jumped and Cayn nodded.

"She is very cute," Cayn replied. Xia blushed. That was the first time Cayn called her cute. Xia wondered if Are walked over just to ease over the tense moment.

"Xia-*pi*, come stand over here," Toi said waving at Xia. Xia walked over to Toi and noticed he was standing on a transportation circle.

"Are we going to Andez on these?" Xia asked.

Toi nodded.

"Yes, unlike the other Organizations Andez is in the air."

Xia nodded.

"I see," she said.

Are and Cayn walked over.

"Xia-*pi* I want to stand next to my *hanev*. Would you mind standing next to Cayn?" Are asked grinning.

"Oh not at all!" Xia said flushed. She stood next to Cayn, red in the face. She peeked up at him. Cayn did not say anything. Xia frowned feeling disappointed.

"Do they know what happened?" Xia whispered while Are and Toi were preparing the circles.

"No."

Xia winced. Cayn's tone was sharp.

"...Are you mad at me?"

Cayn turned his head to look at Xia. His expression was unreadable.

"No. Not at you."

Xia found his answer better than nothing.

"Ready kids?" Are asked excitedly.

Cayn and Xia nodded. In the next second, Xia felt as if she were being pulled from above. She closed her eyes and felt Cayn's arm around her waist. When the tugging stopped Xia opened her eyes to the first glimpse of her new home.

"It's so beautiful!" Xia gasped. Andez was not like Xia thought it would be. There were pillars of stone floating in the air with winged people sitting on them. Large pools of water were suspended in air surrounded by bricks and trees. Xia's eyes grew wide when she noticed buildings sitting in the air. Xia looked up and saw the faintest outline of houses- or something like them. Andez was a city in the air! She looked down and saw the transportation platform she was standing on, but under that nothing but sky and clouds. She did not want to think about how high up they were.

"Pretty, right?" Toi asked. "It never ceases to amaze me."

Xia nodded. This was her new home. A large feather dropped from the sky. Xia caught it and looked at it curiously. It was smoother than silk but heavy. Suddenly, a man floated down from above them. His wings were larger than anything Xia had seen. He was wrapped in white garments and a red sash was tied around his waist. His long white hair floated around his head and seemed to glow in the air. He landed in front of Are and Toi with a smirk to his lips.

"The air smelled sweeter than usual," he said slowly. "I now know why."

Are giggled and gently touched the cheek of the great winged man. The gesture looked friendly, but it was distant in

Xia's eyes. It reminded her of her relationship with Cayn. Xia glanced at Cayn through the corner of her eye then focused back on the new arrival. Even though Cayn was sincere whenever they were together, Xia felt as if he was purposely keeping their contact to a minimum.

I...really wish I understood him better and now to make matters worse... that stupid Jin look-alike had to go and...I'm so mad! Just when things were starting to look up that twit had to go break everything back down! I'm never going to forgive him if Cayn is upset with me! Xia thought furiously.

"It is good to see you again," Are said smiling. Are's voice broke Xia of her thoughts.

The winged man nodded and turned his head in Cayn's direction. Xia jumped a little and looked at Cayn. His face was masked in his usual expression but Xia felt a weariness coming off of him.

"The prophetic child of our people has returned at last," the winged man said. He lifted his hand to Cayn's cheek and caressed it. Cayn did not move. Xia's heart started to beat a little faster.

"I have longed for this day; that we may finally meet," the winged man said softly. He moved his hand to Cayn's hair and ran a few fingers through it. Then he touched Cayn's hair tie and the red-haired Andez flinched slightly. It was almost invisible to Xia's eyes.

"Tell me, dear boy," the winged man started, "why do you not take this out?"

"I have done my all and I can do nothing but wait until the time is right."

The winged man nodded and smiled. He turned to Xia who looked up uncertain. The winged man crouched onto his knees and gently stroked Xia's face. She felt that distance again and it unsettled her. The winged man touched Xia's hair, as he had done to Cayn, and then looked into her eyes.

"Why do you not let your hair down?" he asked.
Xia looked at the winged man confused.

"Because… I was hot…" Xia replied.

The winged man smiled gently and then stood up.

"Cayn, your *hanev* still has much to learn."

Xia blushed embarrassed.

"That is why we are here," Cayn said softly. "I wish to teach if she desires to learn."

Xia was red and looked away from her group. The way Cayn said it confused her, but made her heart beat fast at the same time. The winged man turned back to Are and Toi. Xia looked up to Cayn confused. Cayn smiled at her like he always did and for once Xia felt like a child being babied.

"The building has been prepared. Are you going to accompany them?" the winged man asked.

Are and Toi nodded.

"They are supposed to be *hanev* true, but they are still very young," Toi said grinning. "We'll stay with them for a few days."

"That is good," the winged man said, then turned towards Cayn and Xia once more.

"My hope is desperate for the *hanev* who are to change the world."

Xia looked up at Cayn, confused. He had a saddened expression on his face.

"It is as you have said before, *pi*, she has much to learn."

The winged man kept his gaze level with Cayn's for a minute before nodding once.

"My apologies, Cayn-*pi*," the winged man whispered. "My best wishes for you and your *hanev*."

Xia watched the winged man fly off and after a few seconds began to talk.

"Who was that man?" Xia asked turning her head back to her group.

Are grinned.

"An old friend," she replied. "He is very happy that you are here."

Xia frowned.

"He didn't seem that way," she muttered.

Toi walked over to Xia and placed a hand on her head.

"That is because he is concerned for you two," Toi explained. "He had hoped that you would have progressed further than you had."

Xia nodded but looked away still confused.

"I don't understand any of this…"

"Then tell me why you do not," Cayn said. Xia looked up at Cayn's angry face. Xia felt a jolt of rebellion enter her.

"Okay children, let's not fight until later," Are said relieving Xia. "Cayn be a little more gentle in your expressions. You're going to make poor Xia wish she never came."

"No he wouldn't," Xia said but she doubted Are heard her.

Cayn tore his eyes away from Xia and walked a few steps away. Are followed him. Xia stared at his back feeling concerned.

"Cayn…" Xia muttered.

"Now Xia don't worry about him. He just feels a little angry at himself."

"Why?" Xia asked.

"Ask him yourself. When we get to your house," Toi said. "The four of us are going to have a nice little chat, okay?"

Xia nodded slowly.

"Alright…wait! My house?"

Toi nodded.

"Yes. The home that was prepared for the two of you when you are joined," Toi explained. He smiled at Xia's confused face.

"We will explain it all to you later."

"Okay…"

Toi grinned and gave Xia a gentle pat on the head. He turned to go to Cayn and Are, leaving Xia in her thoughts. She was very upset about what the Raifelle said, but she was especially upset with the Bluse that looked like Jin.

Chosen Sides

Cayn closed his eyes wishing he had more control. He did not even know his face was angry. It all felt the same to him.

Cayn spread his wings enjoying the way they felt free. He walked around his house taking in the feel of it all. This was the place he was to share with his *hanev* after the ceremony. His house was a ceremony by itself with its colors parading all over the place.

Xia was in her room changing. His mother and father had requested that she wear the traditional clothes of the Andez. Cayn was very pleased. He walked into his bedroom, which would later turn out to be the master bedroom. He and Xia would share this room. Cayn sat on his bed and looked out the open window.

Tell me Jin, what can I do to make her happy? Cayn thought as he watched the clouds float by.

I think you're doing fine

I wish I felt that way. I wish I knew how I feel, Cayn thought bitterly.

You are just like her when I first started getting to know her. But you aren't disconnected from how you feel

How can you say that when I just said I did not know how I felt? Cayn thought smirking. *You do not listen very well.*

I heard everything you said, Cayn. I just feel differently. You just feel as if you can't relate to her

Can I? Cayn thought. *I love her more than anything, as you very well know. But I cannot help but think that she and I... will not get to the place I want to be.*

What happened to Cayn? You told her that you would never give up on her didn't you? And you told her that you wanted to teach her, right?

192

You are correct.

Then stop speaking like this. I don't like it when you do

Jin… Why can you not leave me in peace?

Because you wouldn't leave me alone either. I just didn't know it was you until the markings were complete

I did not have a choice.

And neither do I Cayn. Now I would like it very much if you did not keep her so far away from us

I do not wish to touch her the wrong way.

If she doesn't know what they all mean, why would it matter? And if I remember Cayn, didn't you kiss her already?

And I do not feel perfect about it either. Do tell me Jin that that kiss did not mean more than she thought.

She is different from us, Cayn

I know she is different Jin. But I would be the one to feel guilt because she does not understand.

You're such a baby. How about we see what she wants and then go from there

If you think it is the best course, then I shall give it some consideration.

I'd like more than consideration from you Cayn. I want to see it in action

Cayn sighed and closed his eyes for a moment. What Jin wanted was something he was not sure he could do.

To the Andez Jin, touch is worth more than words, Cayn thought. *Can I at least explain that much to her?*

Of course. I just don't want to see you hurting because of this. You want to be closer to her but you have to speak her language in order to do so

What is her language? Cayn inquired in his thoughts.

Touch, Cayn. Just like ours. But the meanings are different from ours. Just hold her hand or embrace her. Use those cheesy lines you said when she locked herself in her room

Cayn glared at no one.

Were they really… that bad? He thought,

Nah, I thought they were very romantic, all things considered

I meant every word I said to her.

I know you did

Cayn opened his eyes again and stood up. His long red hair blew with the breeze that floated into the room. Cayn lifted his fingers to his hair tie and tugged at it until it released the hair in its hold. A stronger gust of wind tangled with his flowing hair and Cayn lifted his hand to remove it from his eyes.

"I wish to wear my hair like this for her. But it is not time now."

Why don't you ask Xia to help you put it back up?

Cayn smirked and ran his fingers through his hair.

"I just wanted to know what it felt like to have it down," Cayn replied softly. "I did not think it would feel so…"

"Pleasant?"

Cayn turned around and saw Are standing in his doorway.

"Exactly."

Cayn's mother walked over to him and took the tie from his hand. She started gathering his hair into a ponytail.

"Your hair is such a nice color, *kanti*. And it is very soft," Are said quietly. "Xia will enjoy running her fingers through it."

"As I will with her own," Cayn said. "Why are you in here *kohnah*?"

"To tell you we are waiting for you," Are said as she finished tying her son's hair into a ponytail. "You look very handsome with your hair down. I wait eagerly for the day where you wear it down permanently."

Cayn smiled.

"As do I *kohnah*," he said.

Are you going to tell her about me?

No, Cayn thought. *Not yet.*

Cayn and Are walked into a large room with floating seats that looked like feathers and a floating table. The floor was clear and Cayn saw the sky under it. He looked up and saw Xia looking at him. She was dressed in blue and green with her hair tied in a bun. She looked beautiful. Cayn left his mother's side and walked to Xia. He forgot about everything looking at her.

"You look pretty," Cayn said softly.

Xia blushed. Cayn found that he liked the way it looked on her. His finger grazed the skin of her cheek.

"…Thank-you," she said quietly. "…You look very nice too…"

Cayn nodded.

"Please sit."

Xia nodded and sat on the feather chair. Her face held a surprised expression when she bobbed slightly in the air.

"This is comfortable," she said grinning. "Come sit next to me."

Cayn could not help but obey. She made him feel happier than he ever did before and he wanted to make her feel the same way. Cayn sat next to Xia and the feather seat bobbed again. Xia laughed again. Cayn smiled and reached out to grab Xia's hand. His fingers almost brushed against hers. Cayn hesitated for a second before taking Xia's hand in his. Xia's eyes widened for a second and she turned her head to Cayn. His heart picked up a beat. Xia smiled warmly before squeezing his hand in return. Her hand was warm in his.

"Now then. Let's start this little meeting," Are said smiling. Cayn knew she was very excited for him.

"Okay," Xia said.

"Ask us anything you have qualms about, *hanev*," Cayn said softly.

Xia nodded.

"Alright," Xia said. "I have a question about what that man said earlier."

"Go ahead," Are said.

"Why did he ask us to let down our hair? Is it important?" Xia asked.

Toi nodded.

"When your hair is tied it means that you are not taken. For people around your age it is normal to be like that but for the two of you, it should not be normal," Toi explained. "...You still don't understand I see. Well let me say it this way. Letting your hair down is proof that you love Cayn and proof that he loves you."

"How is that?" Xia asked confused.

"When Toi took the ribbon out of my hair it meant that I was to be his for the rest of our lives. I had to take one out of his hair too. We are *hanev*. And the proof that you are *hanev* is when your hair is down," Are replied running her finger's through Toi's hair.

"Oh! So the man was upset that we did not take the ties from each other's hair?" Xia asked. "I see."

"Is there anything else you would like to know, Xia-*pi*?" Toi asked.

Xia nodded.

"Yes. So besides the hair thing, something else bothered me about the man," Xia started, "I... mean it wasn't what he said but something else. I see it whenever I look at the Andez... or when I'm with Cayn..."

"What is it *hanev*?" Cayn asked giving Xia's hand a little squeeze.

"Why do all of the people here seem so distant when they come in contact with one another?" Xia asked.

"Distant how?" Are asked lifting an eyebrow.

"Just… when that man touched my cheek, for example. I could not feel the connection I feel with someone else…"

Toi chuckled and Xia looked at him.

"That one is simple," he said. "You belong to someone else. You can't feel connected- or rather he did not want to upset Cayn by being familiar with you."

"But I felt the same way when Are-*ken* touched the man's cheek," Xia said.

"That is because mother is *hanev*," Cayn responded. "To our people touch is valued over words. You do not understand it because I feared touching you too deeply."

"Too deeply?" Xia asked gazing at Cayn.

"I feared telling you too much with my touch," Cayn said in his deep voice. "Forgive me."

"…I do not think you touch me enough to tell me anything," Xia said looking away. Her cheeks were brushed with pink. Cayn slowly raised his hand to Xia's cheek. His slender fingers stroked her face tenderly. Xia inhaled sharply and her eyes widened slightly. Cayn turned her head so that she was face to face with him.

"Perhaps then, you could teach me what it is you would like from me?" Cayn asked. His fingers never stopped stroking Xia's smooth cheek. Xia nodded faintly. Cayn did not know why she looked so faint but he did not think it was entirely bad.

I think she's in shock because you touched her like that

Shut your mouth, Jin. This is not the first time I have done this to her. Cayn thought.

But it's the first time you've done it because you want her to feel it

Xia searched Cayn's eyes for a moment. He felt bare in front of her like that, but it was something he needed to feel for her. Xia lifted her hand to Cayn's hair and touched it softly before hesitantly running her fingers through his thick crimson mane.

"Sure," she said softly. Her fingers still moved through Cayn's hair and Cayn's hand still held her cheek.

"Ahem."

Cayn are Xia turned their heads in the direction of Toi's voice. They quickly let go of one another.

"Oh now, don't mind us," Are said in a singsong voice. Xia blushed.

"I'm sorry," she said quickly.

"Oh no, don't mind us," Are said again. "I found that very cute."

Cayn squeezed Xia's hand and he felt her do the same.

"Are there any other questions?" Toi asked. Xia shook her head.

"Nothing that is too important," Xia replied. "I still want to get used to being here."

"Alright," Toi said smiling. "If that is all, then Are and I are going to fly around the garden. If you need us, call for us."

Xia nodded.

"I will," she said. "But I think I'll be fine."

Are tittered as she walked away with Toi. Cayn watched them leave in silence. He could feel Xia's eyes on him and he turned to her. Her dark eyes caught him by surprise. Every time he gazed into them he found himself willingly a captive to their beauty. Cayn found the contrast more beautiful than all of Andez. Her pale skin only made her dark eyes stand out. It had to be the will of someone greater to have a *hanev* so beautiful.

"Cayn. I was wondering something," Xia said. Cayn was quiet and let her continue.

"May I call you *hanev?*"

Cayn's eyes widened in shock. He was speechless.

Did she just ask… if…? Cayn thought in disbelief.

Cayn say yes!

Cayn had to regain his composure. He released Xia's hand from his own and stood up. His heart was beating faster than usual. He had wanted Xia to call him that for the longest time. Xia laughed softly.

"Please do!" Cayn said turning back to Xia. "It would mean so much to me if you did…"

Xia tilted her head to the side slightly and ran the back of her fingers against Cayn's cheek.

"*Hanev*," Xia started and Cayn's heart skipped at the title, "what does this mean?"

Cayn took Xia's fingers and kissed them tenderly.

"It means 'tender love'," Cayn replied.

"What does *that* mean?" Xia asked curiously.

"The way I am doing it now, it means 'quiet passion'," Cayn said his voice barely above a whisper.

"What does that mean?" Xia asked.

"What does what mean, *hanev*?" Cayn asked.

"'Quiet passion'?"

Cayn chuckled and kissed Xia's fingers again.

"I will tell you some other time."

Xia frowned and stared pleading for him to tell her. Cayn continued to refuse but with a smile on his face. He was happy being with her, listening to her voice, looking at her face holding her hands in his. He was learning more about her and it brought him happiness. If this would lead them to being closer, to being true *hanev*, then Cayn wanted it with everything he had.

∗   ∗   ∗

After spending two days in Andez, Xia already learned more than she thought she would have. Cayn never seemed so normal before and she never felt so out of place but it did not bother her much. Andez was so pretty and everything about it made Xia fall deeper in love with Cayn.

But being in Andez made her think about many things. Xia wanted to know why her Organization thought these people were dangerous, when they seemed to like peace more than anything else. She closed her eyes and thought back to the time when she first met Cayn.

He completely destroyed the two assassins in a matter of minutes. The Andez did want peace, but destroyed anything that disturbed it. The Andez were powerful, but they did not want to use the power they had. Xia figured the other organizations were just afraid the Andez might use the power against them. She was from Bluse, but did not fear an attack from Andez towards her people.

Then Xia remembered how the Bluse tried to kill her.

"It seems they are the ones who fear being attacked," Xia mused.

She wanted to find some way to stop the war that was going on between the Organizations. The war was a dirty war. No one outright killed one another, but sent death in secret. Xia wished she could calm Bluse and Raifelle and show them that the Andez were not monsters. The Andez were wonderful.

"But I guess I'm a little biased," Xia giggled to herself. "Okay, very biased."

Xia sat on the porch of Cayn's house swinging her legs and watching the scenery. Cayn had assured her that if she were to fall something would be there to catch her. She had to trust him.

Trusting Cayn did not take a lot of work on Xia's part. Even though he did cause her fright once and a while, Xia was beginning to understand that his anger was, and never would be turned towards her.

Xia was already in his home, the one prepared for the both of them, sitting on his porch waiting for him to return. The house was very pretty and very spacious. Xia already got lost trying to find her way back outside, which Cayn found amusing. Cayn showed Xia around the house and Xia noticed how similar it was to a home she was used to. The only thing that made it different was that it was in the air instead of the ground.

Are and Toi said that they would stay with them until the ceremony, which Xia still did not know anything about. Xia was going to ask Cayn when he returned.

"*Hanev* are you comfortable here?" Cayn's voice signaled his return.

Xia turned around and nodded. Cayn was wearing a white garment that wrapped around his body tied with a blue sash. He looked more normal than ever.

"I am very comfortable," she replied. "Thank-you for accommodating me."

Cayn nodded and sat beside Xia. She was going to ask Cayn about the ceremony, but to her surprise he got there first.

Cayn spoke in his low voice. "Anything you wished I could do for you?"

Xia's face brightened.

"I have a few questions *and* I have something I want you to do for me," Xia said grinning.

Cayn tilted his head slightly and Xia continued.

"I've noticed a few things… since I've been here," Xia said. "And something's been bugging me about…you."

"Me, *hanev*?" Cayn asked.

Xia nodded.

"Well not really about you, it's about us."

Cayn did not say anything and Xia continued.

"What exactly does *hanev* mean?" Xia questioned.

"To the one who has claimed the rights to me."

Xia stared at Cayn confused.

"What?" she asked.

"It literally means 'to the one who has claimed the rights to me'," Cayn replied.

Xia flushed.

"…It doesn't."

Cayn smirked and nodded. Xia's eyes widened.

"So I have been calling you *that*?" Xia asked.

Cayn nodded.

"Do… you not wish to call me *hanev*?" Cayn asked. Xia shook her head.

"No! I want to call you it! I do! I just wanted to know… that's all." Xia said quickly. She did not want to hurt his feelings anymore.

"Are you sure?" Cayn asked.

Xia's eye twitched in annoyance.

"Stop asking me," Xia snapped.

Cayn chuckled and took her hand in his.

"I have another question."

"Yes?"

"Why… do you enjoy killing people?" Xia asked. Her heart beat nervously.

Cayn was silent and Xia turned her head to look at his face. He wore a thoughtful expression.

"I mean, if we are going to go the peaceful route, then wouldn't you think that killing would be wrong?" Xia continued. Cayn was still silent and his silence shut Xia up.

"I will carry any face if it means I will keep you safe," Cayn replied.

"But do you have to enjoy it?"

Cayn laughed.

"Don't you find a thrill in it when your enemy is defeated?"

Xia pouted.

"I enjoy victory, but not death."

Cayn smirked.

"Then you do not understand that you are entering a world of death. Your naivety will be the reason you are destroyed."

Xia's heart ached at Cayn's words. The edges of her eyes began to sting. Just because she did not enjoy killing, did not mean she was going to be killed because of it, did it?

"But that is why," Cayn's soft voice broke her thoughts, "you are my *han*. Your softness will cushion my fall from grace."

Cayn turned Xia's head toward him and stroked her cheek with the back of his hand. Xia smiled and enjoying the way Cayn's fingers felt against her skin.

"I will protect you from that face," she said.

Cayn shrugged.

"Do whatever you see fit."

Xia nodded and looked out into the open sky. She squeezed Cayn's hand. Something had been on her mind for a while, since she first saw Cayn kill Ren and Lani. But of course, at that time, she would not admit it to herself.

Xia hesitated for a second, but stood up. She shook her hand free of Cayn's and walked behind him. If she wanted to do anything first to stop the war, she first needed to stop the war raging in her mind concerning Cayn.

"If we want to do this, then we should do this right," Xia said determinedly.

Cayn turned a little to look at Xia.

"What do you mean, *hanev*?" Cayn asked softly.

Xia placed her hands on his shoulders to keep him from turning around and smiled.

"I never told you this, but I am in love with the sound of your voice. Not only that; but the silkiness of your hair and the way your eyes look when you say nice things. I love how beautiful and white your wings are and I love how peaceful you look when you fly," Xia spoke while gently stroking Cayn's hair. "And no matter what, I want to do my best to make sure nothing will come between us."

"Why are you telling all this to me now, *hanev*?" Cayn asked.

Xia giggled softly.

"Because I just wanted you to know, *hanev*," Xia said. Her fingers yanked at the hair tie in Cayn's hair. His blood red hair spilled over his shoulders and down his back. It pooled onto the floor in a mess of silkiness. Xia ran her fingers through it fondly.

Suddenly, Cayn whipped around and grabbed Xia by her waist and pulled her to him. She found herself on his lap, staring at him with wide eyes. Cayn's eyes blazed into her own and Xia's heart quickened its pace.

"I... did not finish teaching you, *hanev*," Cayn said quietly. "Is it that you wish to learn along the way?"
Xia felt Cayn's hand in her hair and she smiled.

"That is exactly what I want, Cayn *hanev*."

Cayn nodded and pulled the hair tie out of Xia's hair. Xia found that shaking free her hair was strangely liberating. Cayn smiled warmly at her and then Xia tackled him in a hug. He fell onto his back and his blood-red hair pooled under him. He lifted his hand to Xia's cheek and held it there for a while. Xia closed her eyes and sighed, leaning into his touch.

"What does that mean?" she asked quietly.

"I am in love with you," Cayn replied, "and I want to kiss you."
Xia opened her eyes.

"Do you?" she asked grinning.

"I do, very much," Cayn replied smiling. "May I?"
Xia looked like she was thinking and then nodded.

"You may," she replied.

Cayn smiled and sat up, bringing Xia with him. Both his hands cupped her cheeks and he stared into her eyes. Xia smiled and closed her eyes- ready. She felt Cayn's breath on her lips. Soft.

"I am in love with you as well..." Xia whispered before Cayn's lips were so close she could no longer talk. Xia gripped the cloth on Cayn's shoulders pulling him closer. She felt his nose touch her cheek. She was ready for this. Cayn's lips pressed against her own and Xia melted. She felt Cayn's hands pull her closer and she stayed with him longer than she had ever been with anyone else. Cayn finally pulled away from Xia and she opened her eyes.

"...*Tok han ik Xia*," Cayn whispered breathlessly.

"I can tell," Xia said with a smile to her lips.

*   *   *

"It is hard to believe she accepted him so quickly," Tudios said smiling. She took a sip of her tea, grin never leaving her face. Her husband nodded in agreement.

"It is," he said. "I am glad *quelpi* could do something for Cayn-*kai*. At some point, I thought she would not fully accept him."

"Neisei-*pi*! You had to have more faith! They were destined for one another!" Are said giggling. "I found the whole thing romantic."

"No you didn't," Toi said tapping his wife on the nose playfully. "I had to convince her that what we were doing was right in the first place."
Neisei smirked.

"I believe it," he said. "Are-*ken* was always uncertain about hurting Jin-*kai*, but it turned out for the better. On both sides."
A comfortable silence filled the room. Golden sunlight filled the sitting room. The feather seats let off an orange glow.

"It's getting late. Where did Cayn-*kai* take *quelpi*?" Tudios asked looking down at the clean floor. She watched the clouds pass under her as her question was asked.

"He said he was going to teach her how to fly," Toi replied. "Since she will be living here for a while, *kanti* thought it would be nice of her to grow wings."
Neisei looked surprised.

"Is that not painful?" he inquired softly. "Surely you did not enjoy it when you grew them, Toi?"
Toi smiled and Are laughed.

"Did he tell you that Neisei-*pi*?" Are asked. "Growing wings is like learning to walk. If you fall hard enough, it will hurt but your mother always kisses it better."
Tudios shook her head.

"What are we to make of that?" she asked.

"Xia-*pi* will be fine. Cayn would not let her injure herself unless it was necessary to her growth," Toi said. "...Speaking of which, how are the two of you doing?"
Neisei and Tudios visibly blushed.

"Ah," Toi said with amusement in his eyes.

"*Hanev* I daresay we have made a breakthrough," Are said grinning. "I am so proud."

"Do not be too happy, Are-*ken*. The Organization is not happy about this," Tudios said stiffly.

"Which one, Bluse?" Are asked. "Of *course* they aren't happy about it. The prophecy will be fulfilled in a matter of a few years and they have no idea where their little girl went."

"How are the Inikuria?" Toi asked.
Neisei shrugged.

"They are leaning more towards the Andez's side in terms of the prophecy," Neisei replied. "I suppose it has something to do with the oppression of the Inikuria since Raifelle made itself the unofficial leader of the Organizations."

"That is something that the children will have to deal with on their own," Are said. "Still, it's good that they will have someone on their side. It's unfortunate that the Andez have no desire to fight though."

"Yes," Tudios said. "But Inikuria do not wish to fight in such a dirty war either."
Toi lifted his teacup and stared into its contents.

"I wonder," he started, "if our children will be able to find a peaceful solution to all of this."

"They have to in order for the second part of the prophecy to be fulfilled," Neisei said quietly.

"Not necessarily Neisei-*pi*," Toi said. "The prophecy only says that the world will be changed. But it is only natural that we would want a peaceful solution to all of this."

A tense air floated around the room.

"...I wonder when we should tell them," Are said thoughtfully. Everyone in the room turned to her.

"...I also wonder what they will do. Will they go where they utilize the power given to them after the bonding? Or will they go a peaceful route?" Are finished.

Another silence filled the room.

"Xia... was trained to be a warrior," Neisei said gently. "She may not realize it but it is second nature for her to fight. Cayn-*kai*'s nature on the other hand, is to rely on a peaceful solution..."

"Actually, Neisei-*pi*... the nature of the Andez is not peaceful," Are started, "because first and foremost we are protectors. We... will do anything to secure the happiness of our people. You know this... but the degree to which Andez will go to protect our happiness is something that I can't explain to you."

"Then you are saying that Cayn-*kai* is not peaceful in nature?" Tudios asked.

Are shrugged.

"All I'm saying is that if Xia-*pi* is safe, then everything will be alright." Are replied. Toi lifted his hand to Are's cheek and caressed it tenderly.

"You're beautiful when you're serious," Toi said with an upward turn to his lips. "How can I possibly keep away from you?"

Neisei and Tudios grinned.

"You sure know how to ruin a serious moment," Are muttered. "But that's why I keep you here."

"It still amazes me that the highest daughter in Andez married a Raifelle..." Tudios said sipping her tea.

"Yes, and that you are alive to have children," Neisei agreed. "It also amazes me how the two of you could fall so deeply for one another that it changed our life as well."
Toi and Are smiled.

"You cannot help whom you love," Are said. "I fell in love with Toi- even though he was trying to kill me… We both knew about the prophecy and we both sort of…"

"Fell into its trap," Toi finished for Are.
Tudios tittered.

"That is the way it has to be," she said.

Night came and the skies became quiet. Cayn and Xia returned before dinner and entertained their parents with the events of the day. Xia had successfully grown her wings, thanks to the efforts made by Cayn. Her parents were very proud, but equally surprised that Xia was able to make them so quickly.

"I can't fly yet," was all Xia replied to their remarks about her progress.

After dinner, Toi and Neisei walked out to the balcony for a drink before bed.

"What do you think they will choose?" Neisei asked softly. A gentle breeze mingled with the far away tinkering of bells. Trees rustled in the garden and leaves occasionally floated past. Toi opened his mouth to answer.

"…I do not know," he replied. "I can only wish for their happiness."

"As can I. We have the right because we are their parents," Neisei said. "But do you not have any opinion at all?"
Toi rested his elbows against the rail.

"I know that the Raifelle will try to stop Cayn and Xia from fulfilling the second part of the prophecy. Bluse will too, naturally," Toi replied quietly. "I cannot imagine their lives becoming any easier after they are joined."
Neisei chuckled and rested his elbows on the railing of the balcony as well.

"I disagree with you," he said.

"Why?" Toi questioned eyeing Neisei from the corner of his eye.

"I always thought that love made everything easier," Neisei replied. "I will not stop believing that the two of them will do amazing things together."

Toi chuckled and looked up into the night sky. A gentle breeze graced the balcony.

"I pity the man who suffers Cayn's wrath if a peaceful road is not taken," Toi said. "I will hope that Xia will never see what an Andez can do."

Neisei nodded, hand ghosting over the aged scar.

"Yes. I have only seen it once and I am hoping I never see it again," he said. Toi agreed and together they continued to look up at the stars.

James

The air in front of Fayte and Amalia blurred as James appeared out of the black mist. A chiming rang throughout the room as the mist became more defined. Fayte's eyes traveled down the black rose marking on James' arm to the paper tied with a blue string clutched in James' fist. Amalia stood up, waiting for James' shadow to disappear before she walked over to him.

James' dark eyes swirled with dark excitement for a moment before he offered the paper to Amalia. Fayte knew the look in James' eyes. It was the look of someone's demise- namely the Radicals. Fayte never quite understood by James was so obsessed with killing that particular Radical, when all of those people were evil. James seemed not to care about any other Radicals; they were free to roam and do as they pleased but Cayn- the very idea of that man existing made James' blood boil. Fayte knew that whatever they were commanded to do it had something- *everything* to do with destroying Cayn. If it did not, his eyes would not be nearly as excited as they were now.

"What is it?" Amalia asked opening the letter. Fayte stood up and read the contents over Amalia's shoulder. He frowned.

"What's *Lith ma jok?*" Fayte questioned looking at James. James' face returned to its normal, cheerful disposition.

"I have no idea," James admitted, "but once we find out, we are going to find it."
Amalia sighed.

"We should get started soon," she said. "Raifelle's orders cannot be taken idly."
Fayte sighed.

"Dude, could we just like, take a rest?" he asked walking back to his spot on the chaise and lying down. "We just finished taking care of Lani and Ren's wraiths. I'm still sore."

Amalia frowned and glared in Fayte's direction.

"The only reason you're sore is because-"

"I had to do most of your work," Fayte muttered closing his eyes.

"What do you mean?" Amalia asked, hand balling into a fist.

Fayte opened one eye and stared at Amalia before closeing it again. A smile spread across his lips. James laughed. Amalia bristled.

"I mean that you're so scared of that Radical, dude," Fayte replied after a pause. "You're scared crapless and now you're afraid all of them are going to try to kill you. Not saying they won't dude, but you get what I'm saying."

Amalia's fingers slowly reached to grace her neck. Large blue bruises marred her skin. Her fingers shook and whipped her hand away from her neck. Her eyes were wide with anger and the hand that graced her neck balled into a fist.

"You have no right to speak to your commanding officer this way!" Amalia cried, fingers white. "I am no more afraid of a disgusting dog than I am of you!"

Fayte chuckled and prepared himself for settle down to sleep. Amalia was going to start ranting, and he was in mood to listen to her. Not this time. He was right and that was all he needed to be satisfied.

"Relax Amalia-*ken*," James' soft, smooth voice filled the room. "It is natural for a woman to be afraid of such a beast. He is unnatural and should be eradicated from the world."

James laughed as if he said something hilarious. Amalia turned her anger towards James.

"So a woman cannot fight? Are you saying *you're* stronger than *me*?" Amalia bristled once more. James looked at Amalia with a cheerful expression on his face.

"On no, not at all," he replied. "I am saying that that monster lives to cause fear and bloodshed... and I intend to slay him."

Amalia's hands relaxed and her face returned to its normal frowning expression. James was strange. His expression was cheerful, but frightening at the same time.

"Why do you hate that particular Radical?" Amalia questioned. "Why not hate they all?"
James shrugged.

"He has something I want," he replied simply. A black hole formed under James' feet and he sunk into it without another word.
Amalia scowled.

"We have been working together for a year and I still know nothing about him," Amalia muttered. "Nothing in all the Raifelle records tells me anything that I do not already know and even at my high level of status, records are still sealed to me."

Amalia looked down at the crumpled letter in her hand and frowned deeper than before. She walked over to her desk and smoothed the wrinkles out the best she could before re-reading the letter.

They were sent to find the *Lith ma jok*, whatever that was. Amalia studied the words carefully, taking in that they were from the Radical Organization. That meant that the *Lith ma jok* was up there in the skies. Amalia knew that her small group neither had the means, nor the allowance to make it to the Eracium Radical Organization undiscovered.

Unless James went by himself.

"But that is far too risky," Amalia muttered to herself. James was unstable when it came to the Radicals, Cayn, and the Organization betrayer Xia Chang. Her was far stronger than any of the other people she had worked with, but he also had too many secrets- ambitions that she did not know about. Amalia did not want to rist being discovered by Xia Chang too early in the game and James had a way of being flashy around her.

"Fayte-*kai* I know you are awake. Tell me your opinion on James-*kai*," Amalia commanded, not even looking back at Fayte. She heard him chuckle before he spoke.

"James-*kai* is someone I have no intention of crossing," Fayte replied. "Dude, he was insane in Academy. Every time he wanted something, you could bet your lunch money for the week that he'd get it."

"But why does he have such a fascination with the Radical?" Amalia questioned.

Fayte laughed.

"His hate is as strong as your love for the Radical," Fayte replied.

Amalia's cheeks turned red, but she whipped around to glare at Fayte.

"I have no affection for that monster!" she cried. "I am Raifelle! We are born enemies of that horrid race!"

"Sure dude, whatever you say," he muttered. "All I'm sayin' is that James-*kai* more or less is just like that Radical. That's why he hates him."

Amalia's anger did not go away, but she was intrigued.

"Why is that?" she questioned.

Fayte shrugged.

"Dude, go ask him," he replied. "I'm going to sleep. Wake me up if you need me."

Fayte knew Amalia was furious but he would ignore her for now. Just thinking about James made something inside of him quiver in fright. Somethings were better left unsaid. James was one of them.

Glossary Book I

Bluse Organization

- Mothi- mother
- Fadi- father
- Quelpi- daughter
- Quenpi- son
- Kai- a term of respect for a male
- Ken- a term of respect for a female
- Bavda- love
- Bavdnah- my love, lover
- Pi- term of endearment for both male and female

Andez Organization

- Parkitsta- village temple
- Parkis- high temple
- Han- love
- Hanev- lover, my love, "the one who has obtained the rights to me"
- Pi- term of endearment for both male and female
- Kohvah- father
- Kohnah- mother
- Kanti- son
- Kante- daughter
- Ikelidek- a curse to the Andez
- Tok han ik Xia- Literally means 'I am in love with Xia', but Cayn uses it in a way where the meaning is 'I love you'
- Kai- term of respect for male
- Ken- term of respect for a female

Raifelle Organization

- Kilishthi- a term of respect for female
- Ken- term of respect for a female
- Kai- term of respect for a male

Extra Notes

Xia- Xia
Xia name is pronounced 'sha'.

Xia- Sphereing
Sphereing is most related to the telephone in Hainai District. The boxes that Xia and Jin both had in their pockets are called Mini-Spheres. In *Andez,* Jin is referring to the house Sphere that his parents use to frequently converse with people he does not immediately recognize.

Hanev- Hanev
After Xia asks whether she and Cayn are bavdnah because of the prophecy, Cayn replies that he is hanev by choice. However, he changes the meaning of hanev slightly. Instead of "the one who had obtained the rights of me" Cayn makes the meaning "the one who has obtained the rights to you" emphasizing that he has every right to Xia. Although she did not know it then, Cayn was making sure she understood whom she belonged to.

Whispered Fear- Ken
When Xia is talking to Amalia, she uses ken in a more sarcastic way than respectful. Xia does not mind being disrespectful because Amalia has insulted Cayn.

Whispered Fear- Kai
Cayn does not respect James in anyway, shape, or form but uses kai only because kai is a name to address a male by.

Whispered Fear- That Face
'That face' as Xia calls it, is the 'demon' inside of Cayn that Xia has rarely seen. Cayn insists that he is 'that face' but Xia does not yet believe it.

216

Special Thanks

Thanks also to all my "editors"- Erin Paul, Pryia Phillip, Rike Franklin, and of course my mom.

Thanks to Dember Paige for being my friend through the madness.

Thanks to W.I.S.E for helping me make my dream one step closer by giving me an excuse to spend countless hours writing and saying it was for school.

Thank to Caitlynn Neeson for the awesome job on coloring Cayn! I'm still drooling over it!

Thanks Lulu.com!

Thanks dad and Theresa for helping me get started!

And THANK-YOU READERS!

About the Author

Grace Scott lives in Albany, NY with her mother, younger sister, and dog, Jack Sebastion. This is the first of many books to come.